He didn't know if any woman
had known who he was as a man
without all the trappings of wealth.

But with Dina looking up at him, he couldn't resist the need that was growing stronger. He bowed his head until her lips were soft under his, until he was in the middle of the pleasure that could bring such keen satisfaction.

For a few minutes they lived the desire that was enticingly wrapping around them. But then Dina's hands went to his chest and she shoved herself away.

"No," she said in a low voice. "This can't happen."

"Can't it?" he rasped.

"I don't do one-night stands or…anything that could hurt my son." She looked so sincere standing there with her cheeks flushed, her lips pink from his kiss.

But she was making her position clear and he would, too. "And I'm not looking for anything more…."

Dear Reader,

This June—traditionally the month of brides, weddings and the promise of love everlasting—Silhouette Romance also brings you the possibility of being a star! Check out the details of this special promotion in each of the six happily-ever-afters we have for you.

In *An Officer and a Princess*, Carla Cassidy's suspenseful conclusion to the bestselling series ROYALLY WED: THE STANBURYS, Princess Isabel calls on her former commanding officer to help rescue her missing father. Karen Rose Smith delights us with a struggling mom who refuses to fall for *Her Tycoon Boss* until the dynamic millionaire turns up the heat! In *A Child for Cade* by reader favorite Patricia Thayer, Cade Randall finds that his first love has kept a precious secret from him....

Talented author Alice Sharpe's latest offering, *The Baby Season*, tells of a dedicated career woman tempted by marriage and motherhood with a rugged rancher and his daughter. In *Blind-Date Bride*, the second book of Myrna Mackenzie's charming twin duo, the heroine asks a playboy billionaire to ward off the men sent by her matchmaking brothers. And a single mom decides to tell the man she has always loved that he has a son in Belinda Barnes's heartwarming tale, *The Littlest Wrangler*.

Next month be sure to return for two brand-new series— the exciting DESTINY, TEXAS by Teresa Southwick and the charming THE WEDDING LEGACY by Cara Colter. And don't forget the triumphant conclusion to Patricia Thayer's THE TEXAS BROTHERHOOD, along with three more wonderful stories!

Happy Reading!

Mary-Theresa Hussey

Mary-Theresa Hussey
Senior Editor

Please address questions and book requests to:
Silhouette Reader Service
U.S.: 3010 Walden Ave., P.O. Box 1325, Buffalo, NY 14269
Canadian: P.O. Box 609, Fort Erie, Ont. L2A 5X3

Her Tycoon Boss

KAREN ROSE SMITH

SILHOUETTE *Romance*

Published by Silhouette Books

America's Publisher of Contemporary Romance

To Suzanne Arcuri, my cousin-in-law and friend.
Thanks for your support and for your excitement
in sharing my new pastime with me. Love, Karen

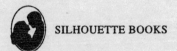 SILHOUETTE BOOKS

ISBN 0-373-19523-0

HER TYCOON BOSS

Copyright © 2001 by Karen Rose Smith

This edition published by arrangement with Harlequin Books S.A.

® and TM are trademarks of Harlequin Books S.A., used under license.
Trademarks indicated with ® are registered in the United States Patent
and Trademark Office, the Canadian Trade Marks Office and in other
countries.

Visit Silhouette at www.eHarlequin.com

Printed in U.S.A.

Books by Karen Rose Smith

Silhouette Romance

*Adam's Vow #1075
*Always Daddy #1102
*Shane's Bride #1128
†Cowboy at the Wedding #1171
†Most Eligible Dad #1174
†A Groom and a Promise #1181
The Dad Who Saved
  Christmas #1267
‡Wealth, Power and a
  Proper Wife #1320
‡ Love, Honor and a
  Pregnant Bride #1326
‡Promises, Pumpkins and
  Prince Charming #1332
The Night Before Baby #1348
‡Wishes, Waltzes and a Storybook
  Wedding #1407
Just the Man She Needed #1434
Just the Husband She Chose #1455
Her Honor-Bound Lawman #1480
Be My Bride? #1492
Tall, Dark & True #1506
Her Tycoon Boss #1523

Silhouette Special Edition

Abigail and Mistletoe #930
The Sheriff's Proposal #1074

Silhouette Books

The Fortunes of Texas
Marry in Haste...

*Darling Daddies
†The Best Men
‡ Do You Take This Stranger?

Previously published under the pseudonym Kari Sutherland

Silhouette Romance

Heartfire, Homefire #973

Silhouette Special Edition

Wish on the Moon #741

KAREN ROSE SMITH's

first book was published in 1992. *Her Tycoon Boss* is her twenty-fifth romance for Silhouette. Spinning stories and creating characters keeps her busy. But she also loves listening to music, shopping and sharing with friends as well as spending time with her son and her husband. Married for thirty years, she and her husband have always called Pennsylvania home. Karen Rose likes to hear from readers. They can write to her at P.O. Box 1545, Hanover, PA 17331.

Chapter One

Damp from the early October rain, Dina Corcoran ran up a flight of stairs to her second-floor apartment. Her mind racing, she fished in her purse for her key. She'd heard of pink slips, and now she knew what it felt like to get one. The personnel manager of the department store where she worked had asked Dina to come to her office at the end of the day. She'd informed Dina that the store was downsizing and they'd no longer require her services as a seamstress. In two weeks she'd have to find a new job.

She *had* to find a new job. Without medical insurance, how would she pay the bills...?

As she inserted her key in the scratched and battered lock, she thought how glad she was that this was the night MacMillian Nightwalker, or Mac as her son called him, had picked up Jeff at the neighbor's after school to take him for fast food and to see a movie. She'd have time to think, plan and look at want ads in the Monday evening paper.

But as she turned the key, she found the door unlocked. Stepping inside the small apartment, she saw immediately that Jeff and his mentor were sitting on the floor in front of the sofa playing a board game.

"Hi, Mom. The movie theater was closed so we came back here. Can we make popcorn and watch a video?"

Dina's gaze shot to Mac Nightwalker and her breath caught as it always did when their eyes collided. With everything that was on her mind, he was absolutely the last thing she wanted to deal with tonight.

His Native American ancestry was handsomely obvious in his high cheekbones, thick black hair and eyes that were such a dark brown they were almost black. She got tongue-tied every time she was around him. He wasn't only tall, dark and handsome there was a sensuality about the way he moved and talked that made every womanly hormone in her riot.

Recovering from her surprise, Dina took a deep breath and crouched down to hug her son. At seven, he was starting to push away from her hugs now and then. But Jeff's asthma made her more protective of him than she wanted to be. "Hi, to you, too. Mr. Nightwalker might have other plans."

The man in question was leaning against the couch, his long legs stretched out in front of him. He was wearing a white shirt with the sleeves rolled up his forearms. His gray slacks had a matching suitcoat, which had been thrown over the arm of the sofa. She could see a silk tie peeking out of the pocket.

He seemed to take in everything about her appearance—from her windblown shoulder-length light brown hair, to her cream tailored blouse and black slacks, down to her well-worn loafers. "I don't have any other plans for tonight. I was going to go back to the office after the movie. The work will be there whenever I get to it.''

Dina knew Mac Nightwalker didn't have to worry about getting fired from *his* job. He was CEO of Chambers' Enterprises, the company his grandfather had established. As grandson of Joseph Chambers, she suspected the man had never had to be concerned about stretching a dollar, or had to worry if there'd be enough food in the house until the next paycheck.

Dina stood and ran her hand through her waves. The wind had been merciless. "Have you eaten?'' she asked, wondering what in heaven's name she could find in the refrigerator to fix that would satisfy a man with Mac's broad shoulders and at least six-foot-two-inch height.

Mac rose to his feet in a quick, lithe movement that made Dina take a few steps back. "We ate at that new steak restaurant over on Locust. Jeff said he'd never been there.''

Hilldale, Maryland, was a town of about fifteen thousand with few choices in restaurants unless you wanted fast food. She and Jeff didn't eat out often. It was more economical for her to cook. Just as it was more economical for her to buy home furnishings from a secondhand store and sew her own slipcovers and curtains. Mac usually picked Jeff up and didn't spend much time in their apartment. Now she tried to see it through his eyes...tried to see their life through his eyes.

Jeff scrambled to his feet. "I had this double-decker hamburger, Mom, and cheese fries, and you should have seen Mac's steak. It was this big!'' His hands made a circle almost as big as a turkey platter.

Mac laughed. "Not quite that big."

Liking the sound of his deep laugh, she looked up at him again, her heart pounding so hard she was afraid he could hear it. Dina knew it would be rude not to make Mac feel welcome after all the time he'd spent with her son. She'd just have to put her worries aside for the next hour or so.

Mac leaned toward the sofa and picked up a bag, handing it to her. "Jeff told me you two were partial to Disney movies. Since I couldn't take him to the movies tonight, I bought these for him."

She'd saved nickels and dimes and quarters and skipped lunches to put together enough money to buy a VCR. It had brought Jeff countless hours of entertainment. "We have videos here we could have watched. You didn't have to buy any."

"Jeff said he didn't have these two."

Seeing the frown on his mother's face, Jeff moved toward the kitchen. "I'll get out the pan for the popcorn."

When he was out of earshot, she said in a low voice, "I don't accept charity, Mr. Nightwalker."

"This isn't charity, Mrs. Corcoran. If I'd taken Jeff to the movies and bought him a soda and popcorn, it would have cost about as much."

She felt her cheeks flush. In the three times previous to tonight when Mac had picked up her son or dropped him off, they'd never actually addressed each other by name. "It's Ms.," she corrected him.

He tried to suppress a smile. "Does that mean you're a feminist?"

His question was a bit sarcastic, his confidence irritating, but then why wouldn't he be confident, with all the good looks and money he could ever want?

"No, I'm not a feminist. I'm a divorced woman who chose to take back her maiden name."

"A bitter divorce?" he asked, serious now.

"A necessary divorce."

There was a compelling field around Mac that seemed to draw Dina toward him, but she fought the force even as she admitted her attraction to him. He was way out of her league...way out of her life.

"I'd better help Jeff with the popcorn," she murmured. Then she went into the kitchen, needing to breathe air in a different room, needing to forget the scent of Mac's cologne and the intensity in his deep brown eyes.

Mac shifted on the lumpy sofa cushion and crossed his ankle over his knee. He kept staring at the video of a family lost in the wilderness. He told himself to ignore the fact that Dina Corcoran's eyes were gentian blue and her voice was as soft as satin sheets on a dark night.

Long ago, because of his wealth, he'd decided he had certain responsibilities to the community and to those less fortunate than he was. A month ago he'd joined the mentor program that the YMCA was sponsoring, and he'd been spending a few hours every week with Jeff ever since. Mac's aim was simply to fill in as the male role model the little boy didn't have, not get involved in his life. And he'd succeeded...until tonight. Dina Corcoran sent his libido into overdrive. It was ridiculous. Since he usually took Jeff out, that wasn't normally a problem.

But tonight, confined in the small apartment, his gaze met hers too often. He was much too aware of her curves and her shiny hair and the freckles on her nose. Since when had he ever noticed freckles on a woman's nose? Most of the women he dated covered their natural beauty with layers of makeup. But then, maybe they didn't have natural beauty. Dina did. Still, he knew better than to get involved with someone like Dina. He knew better than to get involved at all.

Jeff had insisted his mom turn the lights off like in a real movie theater. Only a small, dim fluorescent light above the counter in the kitchen sent a sweep of shadows into the living room. The TV flickered over Dina's profile, and Mac had to stare hard at the small screen so he wouldn't turn his head and look at her. Jeff had stretched out on the floor but they sat on the couch, the popcorn bowl between them. Mac had never seen a woman make popcorn in a pan on the stove. The thing was—it was damn good.

Keeping his gaze straight ahead, he dipped into the bowl again, but this time he felt more than popcorn. Apparently Dina had decided to get a handful at the same time.

For a heartbeat neither of them moved, then she jerked her hand away, murmuring, "Go ahead."

But he said, "No, you can have it. I certainly shouldn't have any room for it after that meal at the restaurant. Did you eat before you came home?" He kept his voice low so Jeff could still hear the sound coming from the movie.

For a moment she looked disconcerted. There was something in her blue eyes, something that troubled him, something that wasn't usually there when he looked at her.

Taking a napkin from the table beside the sofa, she wiped her hands before she answered him. Then she spoke softly. "No, I didn't."

"Did you have to work late?" He knew she was a seamstress for a department store, but Jeff had told him more than once she was always home by five-thirty.

"I...uh...had a meeting after work." As the movie credits rolled on the screen, Dina turned to Jeff. "It's time for bed."

"Aw, Mom."

"It's already *past* your bedtime."

Undaunted, Jeff looked at Mac. "Can you tuck me in, too?"

Mac had never tucked in a child...never thought he'd want to. But something about Jeff's blue eyes, his tousled brown hair the same color as his mother's, made Mac's chest tighten. The seven-year-old hadn't seen his father for three years. Mac had learned that from the YMCA counselor. "Sure, I can help tuck you in."

Jeff grinned from ear to ear. "I'll go get my pj's on."

"I'm sorry he put you on the spot," Dina remarked when Jeff had gone.

"Kids pretty much say what they think and want. Maybe adults ought to do the same."

Dina had shifted the popcorn bowl to the table, and now there was nothing between them except a few inches of sofa cushion. With her looking up at him, Mac knew exactly what he wanted at this moment—to pull Dina Corcoran into his arms, sample her lips and feel her soft curves against him.

Just the thought of it made him rise to his feet. "Does Jeff have a ritual? I've heard that kids do."

"You've never done this before?" she asked with a puzzled smile.

"Nope. I've never been around kids much."

"I'm ready," Jeff called from the bedroom.

Mac was terrifically glad for the interruption. He saw questions in Dina's eyes that he didn't want to answer. They were questions that might draw her into his life and him into hers.

As he followed Dina into Jeff's bedroom, he noted that it was no bigger than his own walk-in closet. There was a single bed painted red and a small chest to match. Both were trimmed with royal blue. An old-fashioned clotheshorse stood in one corner beside three blue plastic milk crates holding toys. A poster of Cal Ripken hung on one wall and an Orioles banner was tacked to a bulletin board that displayed drawings Mac assumed Jeff had colored.

He looked at Dina for a clue as to what to do next. "Did you use your inhaler?" Dina asked her son.

Jeff nodded.

"And you said your prayers?"

Jeff shook his head and scrambled to kneel at his bed.

Mac felt totally out of his element. But watching Dina, he saw that she stayed where she was, so he did, too.

Jeff folded his hands. "Thank you, God, for that new steak place and Mom and Mac. Amen." Then the seven-year-old scrambled back up onto the bed, and Dina pulled up the sheet and coverlet.

Mac moved closer then, realizing he could walk into a boardroom, completely confident, sure of himself in what he had to say. But here in this little boy's bedroom, he felt strangely disconcerted. Especially when Dina hugged her son and gave him a kiss on the cheek.

Mac cleared his throat. "Well...I had a good time tonight. I hope you did, too."

"Oh, I did!" Jeff's head bobbed enthusiastically. And then he got very serious. "I have something important to ask you."

Mac glanced at Dina, but she gave a small shrug that indicated she didn't know what was coming.

"My school's having a special day at the park on Saturday. Dads and kids are going to fly their kites. There's a picnic and other stuff, too. Can you come?"

Without hesitating, Mac shook his head. "Sorry, Jeff. I have meetings on Saturday." And he was glad he did. He only meant to be a role model for Jeff, not a substitute father. But when he looked at the little boy's face, he felt a pang of regret.

Jumping right in, Dina moved closer to her son again. "I'm going to help you fly your kite. We might even win."

"It's not the same," Jeff muttered.

With a troubled look, Dina ruffled her son's hair. "I know it's not. But we're going to have fun. I promise. Now come on, you'd better get to sleep or you won't be able to get up for school tomorrow morning."

Mac walked out into the hall as Dina gave Jeff a final kiss good-night and then turned out the light. In the living room, she headed for the apartment door, assuming he would be leaving now. But she didn't open it.

Instead, she asked, "Do you really have meetings on Saturday?"

It rankled that she thought he'd lied. "Yes, I do." His tone was more terse than he'd intended as he picked up his jacket from the sofa.

As if she hadn't heard him, she went on, "I'd understand if you didn't. An evening now and then is different from giving a whole day to a child."

He drew closer to her until he could see those freckles that so enticed him. "Do you think I wouldn't want to spend the day with Jeff?"

"I don't know."

After they gazed at each other for a few heart pounding moments, her shoulders squared and her chin lifted. He was tempted to ask her what she was thinking, but it was probably better if he didn't know.

Then she opened the door. "Thanks for spending time with Jeff tonight. We both appreciate it."

Formal and polite. That's what he wanted, wasn't it? "I'll call to set up our next outing after I look at my schedule."

"Fine."

Again, the urge to pull her into his arms was so strong he had to fight it, but fight it he did. Then he stepped over the threshold.

Dina Corcoran closed the door.

Saturday was golden with a cloudless, cerulean blue sky. It had been rainy and wet the past few days. But now autumn was declaring itself all over again. Mac parked in the gravel lot then headed toward the laughter of children. He noticed the magnificent yellow, russet and orange of the leaves and wondered why he hadn't taken note of the foliage before today.

For the past few days he'd thought about Jeff and Dina, not sure why he felt guilty. Was it guilt, or genuine desire to spend the day differently than he usually did? Yesterday morning he'd asked his secretary to cancel all of his meetings for today.

His grandfather wouldn't have approved. But Mac had stopped worrying about Joseph Chambers's approval a long time back when he'd known he had to run Chambers' Enterprises his own way...when he'd realized his grandfather sometimes lived in the past. He was a smart old coot and often wise, too, but frustrating as all heck because of his iron will. When he'd retired from Chambers' Enterprises, though, he'd handed the reins over to Mac and stepped back.

Mac's grandfather was the only male role model he'd ever had. Mac knew he looked like his Cheyenne father, Frank Nightwalker, but he'd dismissed the man from his life, just as his grandfather had done. Any man who would abandon his family didn't deserve a second thought.

When Mac reached the park's grassy field, children of all ages ran about, chattered and laughed. Many of them were with their fathers while mothers stood gathered around a circle of grills. Mac shaded his eyes against the sun, searching until he saw Dina. She was wearing jeans and a pink sweater. The wind tossed her hair, and his heart beat double-time.

Because of all the commotion and noise, she didn't see him or hear him until he was practically standing next to her. He lightly placed his hand on her shoulder. "Dina?"

As she turned, her mouth rounded in surprise. "What are you doing here?"

He thought he heard almost-panic in her voice. "I came to help Jeff fly his kite. Isn't that why everybody's here today?" His voice was slightly teasing.

Her cheeks reddened. "You said you had meetings."

Liking the feel of her under his hand, knowing his

fingers were much too close to the ends of her hair, he dropped his arm to his side. "I did. But I cancelled them. It seemed more important to make Jeff happy."

She shook her head.

"What?" he asked, sensing there was something else on her mind.

"It doesn't matter."

"I think it does." He wouldn't let her sidestep him this time. He wanted to know what was going on in her head.

After she hesitated a few moments, she responded, "The other night, I decided you were just a do-gooder. One of the 'haves' giving to a 'have not.' And there's nothing wrong with that," she was quick to add. "Jeff enjoys your company. I just didn't expect you to give any more time to him than you had to."

He'd done a bit of thinking the past few days, and now he took the kite from her and motioned her away from the crowd toward the shade of a few maples where they could talk more freely. She walked with him, and then they were standing very close, gazing into each other's eyes.

"After I left your apartment, I thought seriously about why I became a mentor."

"Why did you?" she asked softly.

"I was fortunate in the way I grew up. I had every advantage. My role model funded charities, but I wanted to do more than that."

"So you decided to give your time, too."

He wondered if everything he'd said still sounded arrogant, if she was once again thinking he was a "have" giving to a "have not." "I didn't have a father growing up, Dina. I didn't have someone to take me to baseball games or play catch or go to the amusement park. That's why I volunteered for the mentor program.''

Suddenly Jeff came running over to them, the soda in his hand sloshing onto the ground. ''Mac, you came! Now we're going to win. I know it.''

Mac laughed. He did that a lot with Jeff and it felt good. Putting his arm around the boy's shoulders, he said, ''I don't know if we're going to win, but we're going to have fun trying.''

Confused by the turmoil inside of her, Dina watched Mac and Jeff walk to the clearing, then drag the kite behind them to let the wind lift it up to the sky. Mac controlled it at first and then let her son take over.

She could hardly believe what she'd said to him. Unlike her father, with his flattery and charm and excuses that covered a multitude of sins, Dina had learned to talk plainly. She said what she meant, and she meant what she said. But around Mac Nightwalker, she'd better hold her tongue. She'd better realize they weren't equals and never would be. She'd better realize her attraction to him could go nowhere. Because of who he was. Because of who she was and what she'd learned about men.

Her father had never been dependable. Throughout her marriage, her husband hadn't been dependable, either. Though it had been three years since her divorce, she still wasn't over the fact that she hadn't been able to depend on her husband, that he'd run out when the going had gotten tough, the bills mounted up and Jeff had been sick more days than he'd been well. She'd had enough to do since then just keeping a roof over their heads, paying the expenses Jeff's insurance coverage didn't pay, and trying to make up for being a single parent. What was she going to do if she couldn't find a job? She could waitress, but that wouldn't pay the bills. Her secretarial skills were mediocre because she'd always wanted to be a fashion designer and had begun working as a seamstress since before she'd graduated from high school.

But now she had to be practical rather than a dreamer like her father.

While the men and boys flew their kites, Dina spoke with the other mothers. But she always kept an eye on Jeff, his inhaler handy in her pocket. He'd assured her he'd used it before they walked to the park.

It was almost forty-five minutes later when the judges decided the winners. Mac and Jeff came in fifth, and Jeff wore a long face as they crossed to her.

"You did a good job," she said.

"But we lost." Her son looked up at Mac as if afraid he'd be disappointed in their effort, in Jeff's effort.

But Mac shrugged. "You can't always win. We did the best we could. I'll show you how to make a kite that's more aerodynamically efficient."

Dina smiled. Apparently Mac was a problem solver. When Jeff saw that Mac wasn't disappointed in him, he smiled again and informed her, "There's going to be a softball game after we eat. Are you going to play, Mom?"

"The mothers are playing, too?" she asked.

Jeff nodded. "Everyone is. I'll bet Mac can hit a homerun."

"It's been a long time since I held a bat," Mac said with a smile. "But it might be like riding a bicycle or a few other things I could think of. You never quite forget how."

For some wild reason, Dina suspected Mac was

talking about making love. Making love. She hadn't been with a man since her husband. Robert hadn't known how to make love, he'd only known how to satisfy his needs. Why hadn't she seen his selfishness before she'd married him? Because she'd wanted a safe haven, because she'd wanted a stable life, very different from the one she'd had with her father.

"So are you going to play, Dina?"

There was a note of challenge in Mac Nightwalker's deep voice. She'd faced a lot of challenges in her twenty-seven years, and she wouldn't back down from this one.

"You bet I'm going to play."

Fifteen minutes later, Dina's appetite disappeared as she sat on a picnic bench next to Mac. His hunter-green, long-sleeved knit shirt hung out over his black jeans. She'd never seen him causally dressed before today and his male impact was no less powerful than when he wore a suit. His elbow brushed hers and her heart practically stopped. As he reached for a hot dog, she noticed how large his hands were, how very masculine, and she realized how long it had been since a man had touched her. What would it be like to have Mac touch her?

Just the thought of it made her stomach tipsy, and she sipped her soda. The breeze picked up, and leaves from the maples blew across the table. One landed on the chocolate cake, one landed on her shoulder. Mac reached around her back and brushed it off. His arm practically around her made shivers skip up and down her spine. His fingers brushing over her sweater sent a flush to her cheeks.

When he looked over at her, he nodded to the paper plate in front of her. "You haven't eaten your cake."

She couldn't have swallowed a bite of it if her life depended on it. Worse yet, she was afraid he knew how he was affecting her and that embarrassed her. She gave a little shrug. "I'll save it for later."

"Are you a chocolate-cake-at-midnight type of person?" he asked, his eyes lit with teasing sparks.

Usually she was sound asleep at midnight—except lately when a tall, dark, handsome man had invaded her dreams. "Are you?" she asked without answering.

"Sure am." It seemed as if the people around them vanished and it was only the two of them, thinking about midnight, thinking about what happened when two people satisfied needs in the middle of the night. Dina didn't know what was happening to her. She'd never reacted to a man like this before. She didn't like it, and it was about time she put a stop to it.

When she hopped up from the bench, her plate almost turned upside down. But Mac caught it, and his gaze told her that he'd felt whatever had sizzled between them, too.

"I have to...to...go see if they need help cleaning up. Just put the lid on the cake when everybody's done."

Then she hurried over to the group of women who were throwing away paper plates and napkins and gathering trash into plastic bags. Dina tried to keep her distance from Mac. Everything about him unnerved her, from his deep voice and broad shoulders, to his intense brown eyes. The problem was, Jeff never strayed far from Mac's side. It was obvious how much he looked up to and admired his mentor.

All of the mentors had been carefully screened by the YMCA and found to be suitable for their program. Still, she'd found out what she could about Mac. But she'd learned even more by watching him with her son. Jeff had been happy since he'd been spending time with him the past month. Mac seemed to enjoy the time he spent with her son. But he always maintained a polite distance. She imagined it was because he was used to a different lifestyle, one that was way out of her league.

A short time later, the softball game got under way and as she watched him come up to bat, Dina wondered if there was anything that Macmillan Nightwalker didn't do well. His stance was confident and easy. Although he didn't hit a home run, he hit a grounder that brought two runs in. After racing to third base, he swept a hand through his black hair and she saw the satisfaction on his face.

Jeff gave him a thumbs-up sign and Mac returned it. Then his gaze settled on her. Feeling as if she'd been under his personal microscope all afternoon, she looked away.

When Jeff took his turn at bat, Mac sat beside her on the bench, the sleeve of his shirt grazing her sweater. She caught a trace scent of aftershave, male and the autumn day. To avoid the distraction of him, she focused her attention on her son.

Jeff took a swing at the first two balls, and the umpire signalled strikes.

"You can do it," Mac called with his hands cupped for magnification. "Keep your eye on the ball."

Jeff kept his eye on the pitcher and waited.

The ball came at him, and with all his might, the seven-year-old swung at it, slicing it. When he saw it skimming the ground between the pitcher's mound and third base, he took off running. Dina watched as he paused at first base, saw the third baseman had dropped the ball, and took off as fast as his little legs would carry him towards second. But as he reached second, Dina watched him bend over and then sit down on the ground. She knew something was wrong. She jumped up from the bench and ran to him, inhaler in her hand.

"An asthma attack?" Mac asked, and she realized he was running beside her.

"Probably," she managed, tears coming to her eyes. She should have known with the excitement of the day and the exertion and the outside air, that this might happen.

When she reached Jeff, she could see the fear in his eyes and could hear his labored breath. She shook the inhaler and gave it to him. He sucked in the medication.

But when she took the inhaler away from his mouth, he gasped and said, "It's bad, Mom."

She could tell it was. Still, they had to wait a few minutes to see if the inhaler would help. His face had a gray cast to it and he was struggling to draw in huge breaths.

"How can I help?" Mac demanded.

"I need to get him out of the grass."

Mac scooped Jeff into his arms, hurrying to the playground next to the ball field. Carefully he set Jeff on the macadam.

"Mom…" Jeff said, still struggling to breathe.

Dina hated watching Jeff suffer like this, but she knew she couldn't panic. If he sensed her fear, it wouldn't help.

But this was going too long. They needed more than the inhaler. "I've got to call 911," she said, scrambling to her feet to run to the pay phone in the parking lot.

But Mac caught her hand, stopping her. ''I've got a cell phone.'' Releasing her, he lifted the edge of his shirt and plucked his cell phone from his belt.

Parents and kids were gathered around them now, and Dina took her son's hand into hers. His fingertips were slightly blue.

After speaking into the phone and glancing at her, Mac snapped the phone shut and clipped it back onto his belt. Then he lifted Jeff into his arms.

''What are you doing? We need an ambulance—with oxygen.''

Mac was practically jogging now, and she ran next to him. With a sharp glance at her, he informed her, ''The ambulance is out on a call. Jeff needs help now. I'll have him at the ER in five minutes.''

She sent up a prayer that Jeff could last five minutes, then ran as fast as Mac toward the parking lot.

Chapter Two

Carrying Jeff, Mac rushed through the Emergency Room doors. Dina ran ahead of him calling for a doctor. One of the nurses hurried to Jeff, took one look at his blue-tinted lips, his ashen face, and hurriedly led Mac to one of the cubicles. Minutes later, the doctor had given Jeff a dose of medication and had begun inhalation therapy.

As Dina sat beside her son, holding his hand, she knew she had to keep him calm to help his breathing, which meant she had to stay calm, too. She'd never get used to this…seeing her little boy struggling for air. He hadn't had a serious attack in almost a year.

She smiled tenderly at him and murmured, "You're going to be fine."

Mac had been hovering over her. Now he leaned down and his breath fanned her cheek as he asked, "Is there anything I can do?"

He had done so much. She didn't know how to begin to thank him for his steadiness, composure and quick action that might have saved Jeff's life.

She shook her head. "This treatment will probably last about ten minutes. Then he'll rest for a while and they'll give him another. That's usually how it works. They paged his doctor. He's in the hospital."

Just then, a man in a dark brown tweed suit, black-and-brown silk tie, and white hair surrounding a bald spot on top of his head came over to Dina and asked kindly, "How're we doing?"

"Better now," she answered with a weak smile, hoping it hid her worry and fear.

The doctor extended his hand to Mac. "I'm Dr. Mansfeld. The nurse told me you carried Jeff in."

The doctor seemed to be asking for an explanation for Mac's presence, and Dina felt herself blush. "Dr. Mansfeld, this is Macmillan Nightwalker. He's Jeff's mentor in the YMCA program. We were at a softball game when this happened."

"I see." The doctor patted Jeff's shoulder. "I'll take a good look at you when you finish with your treatment." The older man turned his attention to Dina again. "We'll check his blood gasses, then decide what to do next. After an episode like this, I want to keep him overnight for observation."

Thank goodness she still had her medical insurance coverage! But she'd only have it for another week. Then what was she going to do?

Two hours later, Jeff, his eyes almost closed, was settled in the pediatrics ward. The events of the day had caught up with him. Dina had made arrangements with his doctor so she could sleep on a cot next to his bed. She hadn't seen Mac since Jeff had been brought up to the pediatrics floor and wondered if he'd left.

While she'd filled out tons of paperwork, he'd disappeared and Jeff had been moved.

Leaning close to her son, she whispered in his ear, "I'm going to get a cup of coffee. Then I'll be back."

He nodded sleepily.

She knew she wouldn't sleep much in the hospital anyway. The caffeine would keep her alert in case Jeff needed her. When she stood, her legs felt rubbery and she realized reaction from the day was settling in on her, too. It was so difficult to be strong all the time. It was hard to take in all the medical information, understand it and then make decisions about it. She never knew if she was making the right ones.

As she left the ward, she felt totally exhausted. She hadn't slept the past few nights, worrying about finding a job, worrying about making ends meet, worrying about what kind of future she could give her son. All of her concerns sped through her mind as she walked down the hall...until she spotted Mac coming toward her. He was carrying a box with containers and cups.

Stopping at the door to the lounge, he nodded inside. "Come on. I brought you supper."

"I thought you'd left," she murmured, his kindness making her throat tight.

"I was hungry and guessed you would be, too. It's been a long time since those hot dogs." He searched her face and to her embarrassment and dismay, she felt tears well up in her eyes.

Not wanting him to see, she turned away from him and mumbled, "I have to check—"

But Mac caught her arm and pulled her into the lounge, keeping hold of her while he set the food down on the table. "What's wrong? Is Jeff worse?"

She shook her head, closed her eyes, and tried to

prevent the tears from rolling down her cheeks. But she couldn't.

"Dina..." he murmured. Then suddenly, he folded her into his arms, and she was leaning against his chest, letting the tears fall.

Mac told himself he should get the hell out of there. He didn't want to become anymore enmeshed in the Corcorans' lives. With Dina engrossed in paperwork and the attendants moving Jeff, he'd been given the perfect opportunity to leave. And he had. But then he'd spotted the family restaurant, thought of Dina in the hospital by her son's bedside and realized he had to finish what he'd started.

Dina was so unlike any woman he'd ever met...and he'd met a lot. He'd dated a lot. But only those in his own social circle. From his teenage years on, his grandfather had warned him continuously about women who would try to marry him for his money.

Mac had learned the lesson firsthand when he'd fallen for and gotten engaged to Maxine Henry. He hadn't seen the gold digger behind the charmingly beautiful and sensual woman until a week before the wedding. That's when he'd discovered that Maxine had ordered a Porsche without telling him and used the credit card he'd given her for wedding expenses for the deposit. That red flag had led Mac to check out his other credit card balances. Maxine had apparently gone on several personal shopping sprees over the phone in his name, too.

When he'd confronted her, she'd batted her long lashes at him and demanded to know if she wasn't worth a few pretty things. He'd bluntly asked her then if she would marry him if he decided to walk away from Chambers' Enterprises and teach business courses at a high school instead.

She'd looked at him as if he were crazy. Realizing he'd guessed her true agenda and he was too proud to marry a woman who only wanted his money, she'd responded, "I never really wanted to marry an Indian anyway."

Why was that memory pushing to the surface now?

After that, he'd concentrated on Chambers' Enterprises and hadn't given a second thought to marriage. It was a union that didn't work and didn't last. He'd never seen a successful one. His sister had divorced after two years of so-called wedded bliss. And then there was his mother. On the few occasions Frank Nightwalker's name had come up, Mac had seen the pain in her eyes. Obviously, expecting two people to live together for a lifetime was an impossible idea.

Dina was warm and soft against his body, and he realized he'd probably let his mind wander to ward off basic urges, which seemed to be making themselves known the longer he held her. If he bent his head, his jaw would touch her hair. He could smell her shampoo.

But as he thought about feeling her hair against his skin, she abruptly pulled away, looking embarrassed and flustered. "I'm sorry. I…everything just seemed overwhelming for a moment."

Trying to slow his accelerated pulse, he stepped away from her and motioned to the sofa. "Come on. Sit down and eat something. You'll feel better."

But she shook her head. "I don't know if I can. My stomach's tied up in knots."

He imagined it would be. On all of his outings with Jeff, carrying the inhaler Dina had given him for that purpose, he'd never really understood how serious an asthma attack could be.

"How's Jeff?" he asked.

"He's almost asleep. I'm going to stay overnight with him."

"Does this happen often?"

"It's been about a year since he had a serious attack like this."

Mac opened the two cups of coffee and offered her one. "Do they always happen without warning?"

Absently she took the cup and stared down into the black liquid. "Sometimes. I should have realized everything today could lead to one—the rain the past few days, the pollens, the excitement. But the alternative would have been keeping him home, and he would have been upset with that. Maybe we should have left before the softball game. Trying to keep it all in balance is a constant struggle. And now with—" She stopped.

"With what?"

Raising her gaze to his again, she said, "I have to find a new job. The store where I work has decided they don't need to have alterations for their customers. Not having work is bad enough, but not having medical insurance…"

Mac saw her eyes glisten again and suddenly he wondered how long she'd known about being let go. Was she telling him because it was a burden she didn't want to carry alone? Or was she telling him thinking he could do something about it? Had she wanted him to get more involved with Jeff for her own benefit?

Damn the suspicions that plagued him about Dina. Maybe she had no ulterior motives. Maybe she was exactly what she seemed—a single mother needing a job.

Avoiding his gaze, she nodded toward the food. "Is there cream?"

"Yes." He handed her a creamer that had rolled along the side of the box.

When she took it, their fingers brushed. The touch of her hand jolted through him like a streak of fire.

After an awkward silence, she raised her gaze to his. "Thank you for everything you did today. You saved Jeff's life."

Mac felt uncomfortable with her gratitude and with the whole situation…with desire for her that he should be able to banish but couldn't. Making a point of checking his watch, he set down his coffee cup without drinking any. "I'd better get going. I have a stack of work on my desk."

"Thank you for staying this long," she said in almost a whisper.

Her blue eyes were soft, seemingly guileless with gratitude. The urge to kiss those freckles on her nose was so strong he had to take a breath.

"And thank you for supper, too," she went on. "I'd like to invite you to dinner one night next week. It wouldn't be anything fancy—"

She was reminding him she didn't live like he did. She was reminding him she was out of a job. The dinner invitation could be an invitation to get more involved in her life because she saw him as a way out. Because she saw him as a way up.

It was time for him to extricate himself *now*.

Rising to his feet, he frowned. "I have meetings almost every night this week."

She looked…disappointed?

"Oh, I see. Well, maybe another time then."

"I'll give you a call in a week or so to see how Jeff's doing. Maybe the movie theater will reopen by then." He crossed to the doorway, then he motioned to the food again. "You'll feel better if you eat."

She simply nodded and murmured goodbye.

He was halfway down the hall when he realized he'd left his dinner behind with hers. It didn't matter. He'd lost his appetite.

It was seven o'clock on Tuesday evening when Mac opened his front door, leaving his car in the circular drive. Possibly he'd go out for dinner before the late meeting at his office. After he switched off the security alarm, he set his briefcase on the low étagère in the foyer. Silence seemed to reverberate around him. At least when Mrs. Bancock had been taking care of the house, he'd hear her in the kitchen or in her suite next to it. But she'd quit to take a job in Pennsylvania closer to her ailing mother.

It wasn't that he missed her exactly. He'd always spent a lot of time alone. But lately...

Dina and Jeff came unbidden into his mind as they had for the past three days since he'd left Dina at the hospital. He'd told himself it was better to keep his distance. They were from two different worlds.

Glancing in the mirror above the curio cabinet, Mac studied his face. He didn't resemble his mother much, or his grandfather. They were both blond with refined bone structures. His mother was about five foot six, his grandfather a few inches taller. From as far back as Mac could remember, he'd known he didn't look like them. Then one day, in the attic, he'd found a box of unusual things, including the picture of a man. Mac had taken the picture to his mother and she'd explained it was a photo of his father. But she'd tucked it away somewhere after that and warned him not to get into the box again.

He'd felt as if he'd done something terribly wrong, as if looking like his father was terribly wrong. Kids in school had made remarks over the years about his being an Indian, a redskin. Once, he'd gotten into a fight. Afterward his grandfather had told him to ignore what anyone said. Mac was the grandson of one of the most powerful men in Baltimore—that was all that mattered.

But over the years, Mac had discovered that wasn't all that mattered. He'd built his own reputation in business and earned respect. Joseph Chambers had always given Mac the impression that Frank Nightwalker had been a weak man who'd walked away from his wife and children; therefore, he deserved no second consideration. Mac had agreed. But every time he looked in the mirror he was reminded of who he was, who his father was. Maxine Henry hadn't only deceived him as far as her motives for wanting to marry him—she'd brought home the fact that he was different. No matter what Joseph Chambers said, Mac was part Cheyenne and nothing would change that.

Did Dina see an Indian when she looked at him?

Asking himself the question disconcerted him. He didn't want to care what Dina Corcoran thought.

Crossing to the living room, he switched on a light. Everything about his house was luxurious, comfortable and of the best quality. His spruce, hunter-green and tan striped sofa and love seat coordinated with the heavy spruce drapes and hunter valances and swag. The oversized, camel leather chair and ottoman and its lighter-colored mate faced the stone fireplace. An original oil painting of a well-known artist's view of the Chesapeake graced the mantle. The house was large and signified the type of dwelling that any man in his position should have. But he didn't spend much time here, and when he did, he was in his den in front of the computer.

Loosening his tie, he lowered himself to the sofa, staring at the phone on the mahogany table next to him. Had Jeff recovered from his asthma attack? Had he returned to school?

Against his better judgement, Mac picked up his phone. After dialing three times, he was worried. He'd gotten a message that Dina's service had been disconnected. Was that a mistake? Maybe Dina's phone was off the hook. Maybe...

Knowing he wouldn't have a moment of peace until he found out what was going on, Mac left the house again and hurried to his car. A short time later, he stood outside of Dina's door and pushed the buzzer.

When he heard her voice call, "Just a minute," his sense of relief surprised him.

After a few moments, when he supposed she'd looked through the peephole, she opened the door, her eyes wide. "Hi! This is a surprise."

"I tried to call," he said.

A young couple with their arms full of groceries came up the stairway then and burst into the hall.

"Come on in." Dina opened the door wider.

"Mac!" Jeff said when he saw his mentor. "Are we doing something tonight?"

Mac shook his head. "I can't. I have a meeting in about an hour. I just wanted to see how you were doing, and I couldn't get hold of your mom on the phone."

"Finish eating your supper," Dina said to her son.

Mac could see a casserole on the table filled with macaroni covered by tomato sauce.

"Would you like to join us?" she asked.

Bypassing her invitation, he shook his head. "I didn't come for supper. Do you know your phone's not working?"

After hesitating a few moments, she finally admitted, "I'm trying to save money in case I don't find work next week. It was either pay for the heat or pay for the phone." Her voice was low as if she didn't want her son to hear.

Mac tried to keep his voice low, too. "You have to have a phone! What if Jeff has another attack?"

Squaring her shoulders, she lifted her chin. "I have to make choices, Mr. Nightwalker. You might not agree with them, but then you're not in my position, either."

Her position. A few more days until she was out of a job. A single mother with a son to care for. "Don't you think we've gotten beyond the Mr. Nightwalker stage?" he asked a bit curtly.

She didn't respond to that question, but instead asked, "Exactly why did you come?"

He took his cell phone out of his jacket pocket. "I came because I was worried when I heard the message that your phone service had been disconnected. You shouldn't be without it and you know it. Take this and use it."

"I can't do that."

"Yes, you can."

"Look, Mr...."

"It's Mac," he reminded her. "And don't let your pride stand in the way of doing what's best for your son."

She looked at the cell phone and then back up at him. "All right. But under one condition. I'll pay you back for the calls as soon as I get a job."

Was she really that proud? Did she intend to pay him back? Or was she trying to make a good impression, hoping he'd offer more, do more?

"Any leads yet?" he asked.

"It's hard to follow up while I'm still working. The tailoring shop in Hilldale doesn't need anyone. I thought about taking in sewing, but that would never pay the bills. I might have to consider moving out of Hilldale, maybe to Baltimore. I could probably find something there. I just hate to disrupt Jeff's school year."

Mac suddenly realized he could offer her the perfect solution. Would she jump at it? Did he really want her nearby?

But then he thought of Jeff and decided to put the offer to her. "I don't know if you want to consider this, but my housekeeper left a month ago. She needed to be closer to her family. I haven't replaced her yet because I haven't had time to start the interviewing process. I need somebody reliable, who can cook and clean and manage the house for me. And I pay well. Five hundred dollars a week, including room and board. There's a housekeeper's suite off the kitchen. Are you interested?"

Stunned by Mac Nightwalker's offer, Dina searched his face, trying to calm her racing pulse. Ever since he'd turned up on her doorstep, she'd wished she'd worn something other than the gray sweater to work today. She wished she'd combed her hair. She wished she could offer him a decent supper. Most of all, she wished he didn't affect her the way he did. She remembered all too well being held in his strong arms, inhaling the scent of his cologne, the excitement being so near to him had stirred up despite the circumstances.

They were standing very close now, keeping their voices low so Jeff couldn't hear. Every nerve inside her was tingling, and she could only imagine living under the same roof with this man, separate quarters or not. She shouldn't be *anywhere* near him.

She didn't really want to be a housekeeper any more than she wanted to be a waitress, even though the money Mac offered was good. For years she had dreamed of taking courses in fashion design. At least if she found another job in a tailoring shop, she'd be doing the work she wanted to do, and that was important to her.

"Well?" he asked a bit impatiently.

She was too tempted, and that was another good reason why she had to refuse. "Your offer is very kind, but I'd like to keep doing what I do best."

"Mending other people's clothes?"

His superior tone irked her. "Are you insinuating that keeping house for you would be any better?"

"The money probably is."

But she didn't only care about money. She never had. She cared more about insurance benefits for Jeff and doing work she was proud of. "Maybe so. But I have some time before I get desperate, and I'd rather find something in my field."

Mac looked down at her as if he was trying to solve a puzzle. He looked down at her as if he wanted more than for her to be his housekeeper. Maybe that flash of heat in his eyes was in her imagination. She felt such a powerful pull toward him.

He leaned toward her as if he were going to…kiss her? But then he straightened. "I have a charger for my phone in the car. I'll get it." Looking over at Jeff who was finishing his supper, he asked, "How are you feeling, sport?"

"Great!" Then the seven-year-old darted a sheepish glance at his mother and Dina knew why. The morning of the picnic she'd asked him if he'd used his inhaler and he'd told her he had. He hadn't. He'd forgotten to use it the night before, too. After she'd given him a stern lecture, she'd wished again that he didn't have to deal with this responsibility when he was so young.

"Are you coming back soon?" Jeff asked Mac hopefully.

"I'll have some time on Sunday. I heard the movie theater will reopen by then. How does that sound?"

"Super. I can go, can't I, Mom?"

Her son loved spending time with Mac, and she couldn't deprive him of that simply because she was uncomfortable around the man. "Yes, you can go."

"Jeff and I can stop for pizza after the movie and bring it back here."

He was being kind again, knowing she was trying to stretch her budget. She thought about being his housekeeper, but then she looked up into his almost-black eyes and felt her heart turn over. Being Mac Nightwalker's housekeeper would be an occupation that was much too dangerous to her heart.

Pacing her small apartment until Jeff and Mac returned from the movie on Sunday evening, Dina went over everything in her head again. The past few days she had examined want ad after want ad, made phone call after phone call, and still hadn't found a position that would pay the bills or cover the insurance she needed for Jeff. She'd even called tailoring shops in Baltimore with no luck. So she had to make a decision. Either she had to use the little money she had put back to tide her over, or take Mac's housekeeping position temporarily.

Yesterday the weather had turned colder, and the temperature had dropped near freezing this morning. Jeff's jacket sleeves were too short, and she knew his coat from last winter would be too small, too. She'd realized that when she bought him a new winter wardrobe, even at a thrift shop, she'd use up a lot of her badly needed reserve savings. The salary Mac had offered was just too good to ignore.

So now all she had to do was find out if the position was still open and what arrangements there might be for insurance coverage.

When Mac had picked up Jeff, she hadn't been ready to ask him if his offer was still open. His job was a last resort. But sometimes accepting last resorts was necessary.

As she heard footsteps in the hall, she braced herself.

Moments later, Jeff was clamoring inside, saying, "Mac had to carry the pizza because it's too big and he thought I might drop it."

The box was indeed large and demanded a good two-handed grip.

"How was the movie?" she asked.

While Jeff launched into a detailed description of the storyline, Mac's gaze met hers. There was amusement there and…and she didn't know what else. She wasn't going to pretend to be able to read this man's mind. She'd drive herself crazy doing that. She also knew she couldn't sit across from him and eat pizza without talking to him about his job offer first.

Taking the pizza box from Mac, she crossed to the kitchen and set it on the table. Then she said to Jeff, "I have to talk to Mr. Nightwalker about something. It won't take long. Can you get out the napkins and the pizza cutter?"

"Are you going to talk to him about me?"

She had to smile. "No, this is grown-up stuff."

Mac heard what she said to Jeff and raised one dark brow.

She nodded to the corner of the living room that was farthest from the kitchen. When she turned to look at him, her words caught in her throat. He was wearing jeans today with a cream colored fisherman knit sweater. He always looked much too sexy no matter what he wore.

She cleared her throat. "Mr. Nightwalker…"

But before she could go any further, he reminded her again, "It's Mac, remember?"

There really wasn't any reason for her to call him Mr. Nightwalker. Not since he'd given her son permission to call him Mac.

"Say it," he commanded her, his voice deep and husky.

Once she called him by his first name, the boundaries would change between them. But he was giving her no choice. "All right…Mac."

He smiled. "That's better."

That was *his* opinion. Knowing the moment of truth had arrived, she clasped her hands in front of her and gazed directly into his eyes. "Is your position of housekeeper still open?"

Chapter Three

Mac carefully studied Dina, wondering why she had declined his offer earlier in the week but was accepting it now. What had changed? Maybe she just hadn't wanted to act too eager. Maybe this was her only alternative.

"What made you change your mind?"

Flushing, she glanced at the coffee table and the stack of opened mail there. "Bills mounting up, for one thing. But there is one concern I have if I take your job. Will Jeff and I be covered by insurance?"

When he'd offered her the job, he'd surmised that would be a consideration. "Mrs. Bancock was covered under the Chambers' employee group policy. You can be, too. There are no pre-existing condition clauses so Jeff will be covered as soon as I sign you up."

"This will only be temporary," she maintained.

She was saying all the right things, and for the first time in a long time, he wished he wasn't so distrusting of women and their motives. What was *his* motive in doing this? To have her close enough to kiss?

No…because he knew distance from Dina was best. His motive was obvious—he couldn't bear to see Jeff lack for the basics.

"However long you need to stay in my employ will be fine with me. That is…if you can cook," he added with a smile.

"Oh, I can cook. Especially if I have an unlimited food budget."

She'd said it as a joke, but he realized that an unlimited budget could be exactly what she was looking for. Still, what happened was under his control. They'd have totally separate lives if he wanted it that way. "When would you like to start?"

"I haven't even discussed it with Jeff yet."

"We could see what he thinks over the pizza."

Her blue eyes were shining, and he saw her swallow hard before she spoke. "Thank you…Mac. I can't tell you how much this will mean to us."

She looked so temptingly vulnerable, so ingenuous. She was wearing a soft blue-and-white sweater today, with jeans. The V of the neckline stopped just above the cleft in her breasts. Had she worn it on purpose? Had she known his gaze would drift downward, and he would want to touch her as much as he wanted to kiss her? Bringing his gaze back to her face, he got lost in the fairness of her skin, those damn freckles, her sweetly curved lips.

"No thanks are necessary," he said gruffly. "You'll be earning your wages. I had a cleaning service in right after Mrs. Bancock left, but I haven't done anything since. Would you like me to drive you over after we eat so you can take a look around? Mrs. Bancock took all of her furnishings with her. I don't know what you'll want to bring."

"We don't have much," she admitted. "My bed, dresser and sewing machine...Jeff's bed and chest."

He motioned to the living room and dining area. "What about all this?"

"Most of it was here when we came, including the appliances. Only the TV and VCR are ours. We'll bring those along."

"Hey, Mom. Mac," Jeff called. "Are you guys ready to eat yet? The pizza's gonna get cold."

Mac nodded toward the table instead of drawing her into his arms as he felt driven to do. "Jeff's right. We can discuss all this over supper."

Before Dina took a bite of pizza, she explained to Jeff that her job at the department store was coming to an end, and Mac had offered to hire her as his housekeeper until she found another seamstress job. Jeff was thrilled with the idea, as well as wide-eyed and enthusiastic, when she told him they were going to go to Mac's house to see if they wanted to live there for a little while.

"Cool!" he whooped. "Mac and me can go to the movies, play catch—"

"Whoa," she said gently. "We're not going to be living with Mac exactly. We'll just be under the same roof. He has his work and his life, and we have ours."

When Jeff looked terribly disappointed, Mac offered, "We'll see each other, though. We'll probably have some meals together. I'm away from the house a lot, but when I'm there, we'll probably be able to work in a game of catch now and then...still go to the movies."

"We won't impose on you," Dina said firmly.

Mac searched her face and then said, "I'm not worried about that."

Dina suddenly wondered if this was the best solution. Did she want to be around Macmillan Nightwalker on a daily basis? On a nightly basis?

When they were cleaning up the remains of their pizza, and Jeff went to his room to pack his schoolbag for the next day, Dina asked Mac, "You said the housekeeper's rooms are off the kitchen. Are they like an apartment?"

"It's two rooms and a full bath. I think you'll have plenty of room."

"Oh, I wasn't concerned about that. I just wondered…"

His gaze unwaveringly held hers. "What did you wonder?"

She didn't know how to ask it except to simply ask it. "I wondered if it was like a small apartment. If the doors…locked."

The flash of anger in his eyes was unmistakable. "Yes, Dina. Both bedroom doors lock." Then he turned away from her to dump the pizza box into the garbage can.

She didn't want to start out their "association" on a tense footing, and she gently clasped his arm, aware of the hard strength there. "I'm not saying I don't trust you. But I don't know you very well."

The creases in his forehead eased. "No, I suppose you don't. You can be as secure as you want to be, Dina. I can even have deadbolts installed if you'd like."

Maybe she was more concerned about unlocking the door herself or inviting him in when she shouldn't.

Everything about him shouted experience and wealth and a life she'd never known. Under his roof...

But she really had no choice. She had to do this until she and Jeff got on their feet.

"I'm sure a regular lock will be fine." She just hoped the regular lock on her heart was enough, too.

In order to have a few minutes to catch her breath before previewing where they'd be living, Dina told Mac she'd drive to his house. Then he wouldn't have to make a return trip. He didn't argue with her.

After leaving the boundaries of Hilldale, Jeff chattered continuously during the five-mile drive about his afternoon with Mac and what it might be like living with him. Dina wondered the same thing.

Mac's directions were easy to follow. A long, paved lane led up a hill bordered by Canadian hemlocks. She could see their branches under the lights placed at intervals along the lane. When the ground leveled, she entered a circular driveway that wound to the front door of the brick house with its stone-faced entrance.

Dina parked her car behind Mac's luxury sedan and got out, her eyes resting on the lights above the outbuildings. There was a garage attached to the house, but there was also another detached garage that looked as if it had living quarters above it.

As they walked up to the front door, Jeff gazed in awe. "Wow, Mom. It's a *big* house."

Indeed, it was.

Mac opened the heavy oak door before they reached it. "Come on in. I'll show you your rooms first. Then we can take a tour."

Dina had never been inside a house so grand, with its high ceilings, custom-laid floors and plush carpeting. When they went through the dining room into the kitchen, the brightness of it made her blink. There was every appliance imaginable, an island in the middle, glistening off-white counters and a large breakfast nook. More windows overlooked the back gardens...at least, that's what she imagined they overlooked. It was too dark to see outside at the moment.

When Mac showed them the two rooms and bath off of the kitchen, she knew she and Jeff could easily be comfortable here and said as much. The walk-in closet in her bedroom was practically as big as Jeff's room in the apartment.

Suddenly fear gripped her. What if she liked it here too much? What if she let her head be turned by appliances and carpeting and the man standing before her, looking too sexy and masculine for her peace of mind? She couldn't let that happen. She had to forge her own life for herself and Jeff...and she *would*.

Mac motioned to the rest of the house. "There's a big screen TV in the family room that I think Jeff's going to like."

"Can I see it?" Jeff asked.

Mac laughed. "Sure, come on."

His arm brushed Dina's as they walked through the kitchen, and she felt as if she'd just downed a shot of her father's Irish whiskey.

Jeff was so entranced with the TV, he asked if he could watch it for a few minutes.

Mac said, "Sure. You can stay here while I give your Mom the rest of the tour."

After Dina followed Mac to the basement, she saw a Ping-Pong table, a pool table and also a workout room filled with everything a man would need to keep fit. And Mac certainly was fit.

She glanced at the Nautilus machine then back at him. "How often do you work out?"

"About three times a week. I wish I could spend more time in here."

When they returned to the first floor, there was a short hall leading to the left. "A person could get lost in this house," she murmured.

"I can draw you a map if you'd like," he joked.

She blushed. Her remark must have made her seem like the original country bumpkin to him.

Walking down the short hallway, he opened a door. When she stepped inside, she realized that this was where Mac Nightwalker spent his time when he was at home. This was where he felt comfortable.

The room was different than all the others. It was paneled in knotty pine, and bookshelves lined one wall. There was a leather sofa in navy and a matching chair behind the huge desk. But it was the pictures on the walls that caught her eye. All of them looked like scenes from the Old West. The paintings were sepia, one of Native American braves, another of wild horses, another of a landscape with teepees in the distance. Enhancing the western feel, a set of three bronze mustangs sat on the desk.

"I like this room."

"Because it's different?"

There was something in his voice, and she almost felt as if his bringing her in here was some kind of test.

"No, because it's warm. I have the feeling you spend a lot of time in here. There's a comfortable spirit about it."

When he moved closer to her, tingles skipped up and down her spine. He glanced at the pictures on the wall, then back at her. "I'm Cheyenne. At least my father was. I don't know very much about him or his background. Actually, I know nothing at all except that he *was* Cheyenne."

"He's deceased?" she asked gently.

"I don't know if he is or not."

When they'd entered the room, Mac had flipped a switch that lit up the wrought-iron sconce lights on the wall. The illumination was dim, giving the den an intimate feel. Mac's gaze swept over her face as they stood there, and then rested on her lips.

Drawing some air into her lungs, trying to keep her focus on the conversation, not the vibrations thrumming between them, she responded, "That must be hard for you."

He shook his head. "That's just the way it is."

She suspected there was a lot he wasn't saying, pain he didn't want to share, privacy he wanted to keep.

But thoughts of Mac and his father soon fled as he bent his head and his lips hovered over hers.

She thought about running back to her apartment, but didn't, because she longed to taste his kiss.

The firm heat of his lips was more seductive than she'd ever dreamed. This kiss was so different from any she'd ever had. The few boys she'd kissed before her marriage had only used kissing as a means to an end, an end she'd denied them because she'd intended to wait until she was married. Robert hadn't liked kissing. Mac's kiss was an entity of its own…sensual and slow and exciting in its restraint.

Then suddenly his arms surrounded her and the restraint vanished. He moved his mouth over hers, coaxing her lips apart, making her tremble with a need she didn't know she still had.

She couldn't help but open her lips and receive him. She couldn't help but want more. His tongue explored her mouth, making her knees shake and her arms go around his neck. He was so solid, so strong, so…much a man. His tongue was hungry and for the first time in her life, she felt as if someone else controlled every sensation in her body, that she was simply going along for the ride, that she wanted to let go and soar away to a place where she didn't have to worry about responsibility. The hunger transformed into a need that she felt in him, too. It was foreign and dark and thrilling.

But then abruptly Mac broke the kiss, lifted his head and stepped back.

There was something in his eyes she didn't like. Wariness? Why would he be wary of her?

"I shouldn't have done that," he said brusquely.

Pride made her square her shoulders and look him in the eye. "Why shouldn't you have done that?" Even though deep in her bones she knew the answer, the question blurted out before she could grab it back.

"Because you're coming here to work for me, Dina, nothing else. I told you you'd be safe, and I don't want you to have any doubts about that."

Employer, employee. He was getting their roles straight, drawing the line where he wanted it. Well, that's where she wanted it, too. "You're right, of course."

She deliberately checked her watch, still trying to calm the racing beat of her heart. She was determined to show Mac the kiss hadn't affected her anymore than it had affected him. "I'd better get Jeff home. He has school tomorrow. My landlord has a truck. Maybe he'll let me borrow it and help me load the furniture. When would you like me to move in?''

''Chambers' has several trucks. We can use one of those. Do you want to move while Jeff's in school?''

''I don't want to disrupt your schedule. There isn't much to pack, but I do have to store a few things in boxes.''

''How about tomorrow afternoon then?'' he asked. ''Give me a call when Jeff gets home from school. We can make one or two trips and you'll be settled in by tomorrow night.''

Tomorrow night...under the same roof as Mac.

She was still reeling from his kiss and couldn't imagine her response if he touched her more intimately. She'd probably melt in his arms. But it was obvious that wasn't what he wanted—and she didn't, either. Her life was complicated enough. She would concentrate on making a temporary home here for her and Jeff, and doing the best job she could of housekeeping.

''Tomorrow afternoon will be fine,'' she said in answer to his question.

Forcing herself away from Mac's magnetic pull, she crossed to the door. While she was living here, she would just have to remember she didn't belong here. This was Mac Nightwalker's world, and she'd better not forget it.

The following evening, while Dina stood in the doorway, Mac shifted Jeff's bed to the wall where she'd said she wanted it. She'd never expected Mac to help her arrange furniture after moving it. But he'd insisted, saying it was too heavy for her to handle. Little did he know that she'd moved everything to the apartment by herself after she'd left the house she'd shared with Robert. There'd been no one to help her, and she'd learned many years ago to do what she had to do. Responsibility had made her resourceful.

She and Mac hadn't talked further about what had happened the night before. There really hadn't been time for them to talk about anything. But the memory of their kiss was still vivid in Dina's mind. There would be no forgetting the way she'd felt in Mac's arms, under his lips, in the midst of his passion.

Jeff came into the room then and tugged on her elbow. He asked in a low voice, "I'm hungry, Mom. Can I open the refrigerator and see what's inside?"

Overhearing, Mac came over to him and crouched down before him. "I know all of this is a little confusing for you, but I want you to feel at home here. Consider the kitchen and the family room your territory. You can eat whatever you want, you can watch the TV or play the stereo whenever you want. Okay?"

Jeff looked up at his mom and she nodded. "Okay."

"There are apples in the refrigerator. Why don't you have one of those until we decide what we're going to do for supper," Mac suggested.

Jeff took off for the kitchen.

"I can make something," Dina said, "...as soon as I find my way around."

"Mrs. Bancock kept the freezer well stocked, but there won't be time to thaw anything now."

"That's not a problem. I can be creative. Do you have eggs, cheese, flour?"

"Probably. What do you have in mind?" His dark eyes never left her face and she felt self-conscious. After packing and moving, her hair was probably mussed and the dash of lipstick she'd applied long gone.

"An omelet and pancakes."

"I don't know if there's pancake mix. I'm rarely here for breakfast."

She had the feeling Mac had never learned his way around a kitchen. "I don't need pancake mix. My dad taught me a made-from-scratch recipe when I was a little girl so I could make them for him."

"So you could make them for him? Where was your mom?"

Her mother had cleaned other people's houses and had brought in a steady stream of income. On the other hand, her father had hopped from one job to the next, always looking for something better, having plenty of time off between jobs for poker games and having a beer with friends. After her mom died, Dina had pretty much taken care of herself.

"Mom died when I was eleven. After that, I learned to cook and made supper a lot when Dad didn't bring something home."

"Where's your dad now?"

"Last time I talked to him, he was piloting charter boats in Florida for fishing excursions."

"You don't talk to him often?"

Dina wanted to end this conversation. But she'd like to know more about Mac. The only way that would happen was if she told him more about herself. "Dad doesn't have a phone where he's staying, so he calls me. I have a P.O. box number for him. I'll have to write and tell him we're here. He's pretty much a free spirit and doesn't stay in one place very long."

Mac's dark eyes searched her face as if he knew

there was more she wasn't telling him. "It sounds as if you had a lot of responsibility early."

She shrugged. "A lot of freedom, too. And maybe it was a good thing. It prepared me for—" She stopped. She didn't want to get into that.

But Mac was perceptive. "For after your divorce?"

Nodding, she added, "And everything I've gone through with Jeff."

Mac motioned to the small appliance with tubes and a mouthpiece that he'd carried in, now sitting on the chest. "What's that?"

"It's a nebulizer, a breathing machine. After this last attack, Jeff had to use it three times a day, but now he's off of it again."

"You've had a rough life, haven't you?"

The last thing she wanted was for Mac to feel sorry for her. "Not as rough as some. I always knew Dad loved me. And I have Jeff. His hugs at night make up for almost anything."

Mac was studying her again. It was a probing examination that made her feel uncomfortable.

Moving away from him, she crossed to the boxes along the wall. "I'll unpack Jeff's things and then see what I can find in the kitchen."

When Mac left the room, she breathed a sigh of relief.

A short time later, Dina was peeking in cupboards and drawers, finding everything she needed, when Jeff pulled out the stool at the counter near the telephone and hiked himself up onto it.

"Do you know where my dad is?" he asked.

The question stunned Dina. She'd come home from work one day after picking up Jeff at day care when he was four and found a note. Robert had said he was leaving to start a new life. She'd never seen him again. Jeff had never really asked her questions about his father before, so she hadn't had to make explanations.

Recovering her composure, she answered him truthfully, "No, I don't know where he is. Is there a particular reason you'd like to know?"

"It's just... Other kids' moms and dads are divorced, but they see their dads. I don't see mine. I don't even remember what he looks like."

That was true. After Robert's abandonment, Dina had torn up and thrown away every picture she'd had of him.

Dina caught sight of Mac standing in the kitchen doorway then, and she wondered how much he'd heard.

Coming inside after putting the truck in the detached garage, Mac had seen Jeff going into the kitchen. He'd found a baseball mitt in one of the boxes in storage in the garage and had thought the boy would like to use it. But now the mitt became secondary. Mac realized *exactly* how Jeff felt. He was different from the other kids, and he didn't like the feeling.

Mac had experienced the same thing. Not because his father was gone—Joseph Chambers had always been a stand-in—but because he had Cheyenne blood.

Now he crossed to Jeff with the mitt in his hand. His eyes caught Dina's, and he wondered what kind of relationship she'd had with her husband, what had happened between them, why Jeff didn't remember what his father looked like.

"I don't know where my father is, either," he said gruffly.

Jeff's eyes went wide. "Why not? Is he like grandpa? Does he go everywhere?"

"No. He went away when I was a kid and never came back." But Mac suddenly realized he hadn't asked the questions that Jeff was asking now. He'd taken Joseph Chambers's word that his father had been a weak man who hadn't cared about his wife or his son and daughter.

"Jeff's dad left when he was four," Dina explained.

"It looks as if we have something in common."

Jeff nodded seriously.

Handing him the catcher's mitt, Mac ruffled his hair. "I found this in my garage. Think you'd like to use it?"

"Sure would. Can we go out now?"

Dina smiled indulgently. "It's dark outside now."

"Tomorrow?" Jeff asked Mac.

"Sure. I'll try to get home before the sun goes down."

"I put your clothes on your bed," Dina said. "Why don't you put them in the drawers so you know exactly where they are."

Jeff punched the mitt, right hand into left, and then hopped off the stool. "Okay."

When Jeff was out of earshot, Mac asked, "You really don't know where his father is?"

"No, I don't," she said, her voice clipped. Then she sighed. "I was so angry after he left, I tore up every picture I had of him. I shouldn't have done that, I guess."

"Why did Jeff's dad leave?" It was none of his business and she was probably going to tell him that, but he wanted to know anyway.

After a long stretch of silence, she sank down onto the stool her son had vacated. "When Jeff was born, I was twenty. Robert was twenty-three. I'd been ecstatic when I found out I was pregnant. But Robert wasn't. After Jeff was born, he developed a problem with the asthma. Robert liked that even less.''

She shook her head. ''Visits to the Emergency Room and the doctor became frequent. Bills piled up. One day when I came home from work after picking up Jeff at day care, Robert was gone. A few weeks later his lawyer served me with divorce papers. I signed them, took back my maiden name for both of us, and tried not to look back.''

Mac couldn't understand men who walked out on their children. Didn't they have any sense of responsibility? Any sense of what being a man truly meant? ''What about child support?''

''Maybe it was foolish, but I signed it away. I didn't want to take anything from Robert when he didn't want to be married to me and didn't want his son.''

Considering Dina's situation, Mac asked, ''Do you regret that now?''

She thought about it. ''Most of the time I don't. When I lost my job...'' She bit her lower lip. ''Like I said, there's no point looking back.''

Dina had known responsibility early and had become very practical. Had she been practical by accepting his job offer? Was it merely a stopgap measure? Or did she plan on turning it into more?

She'd been so responsive last night. He'd kissed a lot of women, but usually he was the one with the hunger and the basic need. Last night he thought he'd felt that need and hunger in Dina, too. Was she that sensual a woman? Did desire run hot in her blood as it sometimes ran hot in his? Or was she simply being practical again, taking his kiss and turning it into something they'd both remember? In a way he'd been testing her. Yet he'd gotten much too caught up in it...in Dina.

"I have resources at my disposal and I could probably find your ex-husband for you if that's what you want." Child support could solve some of her problems.

She seemed to mull it over. "If I thought contacting Robert would do any good, if I thought it would be good for Jeff... I suppose it's possible he's had a change of heart since our divorce. I've never really considered it before. Maybe he *would* like to get to know his son. If so, I should put my feelings aside."

Her feelings? Could she still have feelings for the man? Or did she mean her animosity toward him? "You'd like me to try to find him?"

He could tell she was examining the idea, and finally she said, "Yes. If you can, I'll decide what to do next." Then she stood and looked up at him. "Why haven't you tried to find *your* father?"

"My father abandoned me and my sister. He walked away without a second glance. I don't want anything to do with him."

"Jeff's father abandoned him, too," she said softly. "But that doesn't keep him from wanting to know him."

Mac frowned. He wanted to be a mentor to Jeff and to keep it at that. He'd never expected Dina and her son to stir up his life, to stir up questions he'd never answered. But they were.

And he didn't like it.

Chapter Four

Dina was dusting Mac's living room when the photo album under the coffee table caught her eye. She ignored it at first, keeping her mind on the task at hand. She hadn't realized exactly how large Mac's house was until she'd actually started cleaning it. After she'd taken Jeff to school this morning, she'd made a pineapple upside-down cake to go with the ham she'd taken from the freezer last night. Then she'd decided to give the whole house a once-over before she thoroughly cleaned it room by room. At three-thirty she'd picked up Jeff at school, put the ham in the oven and tried to finish up for the day. Now Jeff was sitting at the kitchen table working on his homework.

Her gaze went back to the photo album.

Pulling it out, she set it atop the coffee table while she knelt in front of the sofa and opened it. Most of the first pages were filled with pictures of two children, and Dina guessed they were Mac and his sister. He looked to be about five and the girl was younger.

His sister took after his mother and grandfather. Although she had dark brown hair and dark brown eyes, her features were delicate like her mother's.

"Learning anything?" a deep voice asked, startling Dina.

She felt a little guilty for going through the pictures, yet they hadn't been hidden away. "Just that you and your sister must have spent a lot of time together."

"Suzette's two years younger than I am and was a constant tagalong as I was growing up."

Dina had paged about halfway through the album and now pointed to a high school picture of his sister. "She's beautiful."

"Yep, and she knows it, too," Mac said with some amusement. "Much to my grandfather's chagrin, she had boys calling her when she was fourteen." He pointed to a group photograph apparently done by a photographer. "My grandfather arranged to have that picture taken after my college graduation."

"He's frowning," Dina commented.

Mac laughed. "Grandfather's usually frowning about something. That day Suzette had announced she was getting engaged. Grandfather didn't approve of her choice. And he turned out to be right. Two years after they married, Suzette and Trent were divorced."

"You respect his opinion?"

"He made Chambers' Enterprises what it is today. He's stubborn, with a will like steel. So where my MBA left off, he took over."

Dina had always nurtured dreams of going to fashion design school some day...of becoming a successful designer. What would it be like to have a goal and be able to head for it straightaway without detours? It seemed Mac had done that with his life.

Closing the photo album, she replaced it under the coffee table. "I didn't mean to pry. I was just curious."

Mac's gaze went to the dust cloth on the table and the sweeper leaning against the armchair. "Did you have trouble finding anything today?"

Last evening he'd shown her where the utility closet was located. "No. Your housekeeper kept a very tight ship. Everything's in its place. I aired out the guest bedrooms upstairs and tried to do a quick once-over through the whole house. Tomorrow I'll start room by room and do a more thorough job. But I..."

She hesitated. "I didn't do your bedroom. I didn't know if you wanted me to...go in there, I mean."

"It's part of the house. There's no reason why you shouldn't."

She had stepped into his bedroom and then stepped right out again. It had seemed too intimate going inside where she'd glimpsed a king-size bed, jeans hung over a chair arm, a cable knit sweater on the cedar chest. They hadn't really delineated her duties. "I'll do laundry tomorrow. Is there a hamper in your room?"

"I send my shirts to a laundry and most of the rest is dry cleaned. But there is a hamper inside my walk-in closet for...other things."

Boxers? Briefs? Better she didn't think about what he wore under his trousers.

They both knew what she'd be washing and the idea of it seemed almost too intimate. His gaze was steady on hers, and she remembered their kiss and wondered if he was remembering it, too. Rising to her feet, she smelled a hint of his cologne. He'd tugged down his tie and opened the top button of his shirt. He looked as sexy as a man could look, and her whole body seemed to tingle, even though she stood a good foot away from him.

"I'd better check on supper," she said and would have slipped past him, but he caught her arm.

His clasp was firm, and she knew there was strength in Mac Nightwalker that went even deeper than his muscled physique. When she looked up at him, she almost swayed toward him, but she caught herself.

"I have something for you." His voice was low and husky. The look in his eyes made everything inside her riot.

"What?"

Releasing her arm, he reached into his inside jacket pocket and pulled out a slip of paper. "I have Robert Craft's address and phone number."

"Already?"

He shrugged. "With the name, birth date and social security number, it's fairly easy to obtain information." He held it out to her.

She didn't take it right away because she wasn't sure what she was going to do with it. Then knowing what trouble he'd gone to, she slid it from his fingers. Her hand didn't touch his. His hand was so much larger than hers. And last night in her dreams...

Feeling a flush come to her cheeks she murmured, "Thank you."

"Are you going to call him now?" Mac asked.

"Oh no. I mean...I need to think about it. To think about what I'd say. We haven't spoken in three years."

"I got more than his address," Mac admitted. "He hasn't remarried. He's an accountant with a computer company in Dayton."

Now she glanced at the address. Ohio. If Robert did want to see Jeff, it wouldn't be impossible. "As I said, I have to think about what I want to say to him."

There was a look on Mac's face she didn't understand. It was very intense, very probing. "Jeff seems to have settled in."

"He likes the idea that I'm going to pick him up at school and that he doesn't have to take the bus home or stay with the neighbor."

"I think it's important for kids to know their parents are available if they need them."

"That's all too true," Dina responded, thinking about her dad.

While she was growing up, she'd never known exactly when he'd be home or where he'd be. But when he *had* been there, he'd made her laugh, and he'd made her feel safe. The problem was, she'd never been able to depend on him to be there for her when she needed him. Not as a child and not as an adult. Just as she hadn't been able to depend on Robert.

And Mac...?

She shouldn't even think about depending on him at all. But when he looked at her as he was looking at her now...

"The house smells good," he said. "I'd almost forgotten what it was like to come home to a meal. Most nights I worked late and Mrs. Bancock left me casseroles or something I could warm up."

"If you let me know when you're working late, I can hold dinner and feed Jeff earlier. Are we all going to eat...together?" She didn't know what the protocol was going to be.

"It would seem silly for me to eat by myself in the dining room, wouldn't it?"

"I know. But it's not as if we're a family. You'll have to tell me what to expect."

"I expect I'll enjoy your company and Jeff's at dinner."

She wondered what kind of relationships Mac had had in the past...if he'd ever shared his life with someone. But that seemed much too personal to ask. They stood there close together, seemingly bound by something Dina didn't understand. Was it simply chemistry?

It might be chemistry but there was nothing simple about it.

Stepping away from him, she murmured, "I really have to check on that ham." And she left him in his living room, feeling as if she'd escaped a temptation too great to ignore, yet also sorry about that, too.

It was almost nine o'clock when Dina picked up the phone in her bedroom to call her ex-husband. After supper, Mac had said he would be in his office working for the rest of the evening. Jeff had watched TV on the big screen in the family room while she'd put away the sweeper and tidied up, thinking about her ex-husband, about what she might say. There was no point in putting it off. This was something she had to do for Jeff's sake.

The phone rang twice and then a man whose voice was no longer familiar picked it up. "Hello?"

"Robert?" she asked tentatively.

"Who is this?" he demanded.

"It's Dina Corcoran."

There was silence, and she wondered if he was going to hang up on her, but he didn't. He asked gruffly, "What do you want?"

"I'm fine, and I hope you are, too," she said sweetly, emphasizing his rudeness.

"I'm great. But don't try to fool me, Dina. This isn't a social call. Not after all these years. What do you want?"

His curt and almost angry tone annoyed her. "I want to know if you've changed your mind about being involved in Jeff's life. We've moved temporarily and if you want to keep track of him—"

"I have another life now, Dina. I'll be getting married again in the spring. Debby has three kids, and they're more than enough for me to handle."

"How are you going to handle three when you couldn't cope with one?" Dina asked, remembering all the times Robert had abdicated his responsibility as a parent.

"I'm older now. I have a better job, and Debby doesn't expect me to take care of her children for her. She knows they're *her* problem."

Dina couldn't imagine marrying a man who didn't want to share parenthood completely, but then that's why Robert had left. She should have realized he wouldn't have changed. Still, for Jeff's sake... "Are you telling me that you intend to cut Jeff out of your life forever?"

"He wouldn't even know me."

"He would if you'd let him."

"Look, Dina. I don't want to stir things up."

"Would a phone call or a note every once in a while be so difficult? He's your son, Robert."

"You're looking for child support, aren't you? You signed papers, Dina. You're not getting it out of me now. Or college tuition later."

"I don't want anything from you, except some consideration for your son. Can't you at least think about calling him, getting to know him a little bit, even if it's long distance? He's asking questions.''

''And I'm sure you've filled him in with the appropriate answers.''

''I haven't known what to tell him. The only thing he knows is that you left and never came back.''

''He was too young to know the difference.''

''He was four. He knew he had a father one day and the next day he didn't.''

Robert's silence led Dina to believe he was thinking it over.

''He's in bed now. But he's usually awake until around eight. Let me give you the phone number.'' She rattled it off once and then again more slowly, hoping he was taking it down, hoping he'd call.

''I'll think about it,'' he said tersely.

But when she hung up a few moments later, she wondered if he would, or if he'd simply said that to get her off the line.

After the call, she paced her room. Maybe phoning Robert had been a mistake. Maybe resurrecting the past was a very bad idea.

In his den, Mac sat at his desk looking over Chambers' Enterprises third quarter report. But his analysis hadn't gotten very far. He kept seeing Dina's face as she stood before him this afternoon, kept remembering the taste of her, kept reliving how soft and pliant she'd felt in his arms. Had she called her ex-husband?

Why should he care if she had?

The problem was, he *did* care. He didn't like the idea of Dina and Robert Craft having some kind of connection. Would talking to him stir up old fires?

What if Craft had changed during the past few years? What if he regretted leaving?

The soft rap on Mac's office door alerted him to Dina's presence. "Are you busy?" she asked tentatively.

Not busy enough to get her out of his head. "Come on in. Is Jeff asleep?"

"About an hour ago. I...I just called Robert."

Mac felt the muscles in his shoulders tense. "And?"

"And he says he has a life now. He's getting married in the spring and his fiancée has three kids."

Mac felt relief wash over him, and in spite of himself was pleased by Dina's lack of connection to her husband. Still, he did feel bad for Jeff. "Craft still doesn't want anything to do with you or Jeff?"

"It sounds like that." She said it with a sigh. "But I tried to convince him he owes Jeff something, even if it's just a card or a note or a phone call once in a while. He said he's going to think about calling. But I'm not going to mention anything to Jeff in case it doesn't happen."

Standing, Mac came around his desk and leaned a hip on the edge of it. "I think that's wise. You wouldn't want to get his hopes up just to have them dashed."

She looked so soft and vulnerable standing there.

He asked, "That call was hard for you, wasn't it?"

When she nodded, her eyes became shiny.

"Dina..." he said gently.

But she just shook her head and turned away from him, taking a few steps toward the door.

Panic surged through him. Was she still in love with her ex-husband? He straightened quickly, caught her arm and nudged her around. "What is it? What did he say?"

"It...it wasn't anything he said. Actually it was everything he *didn't* say. I never understood how he could walk away like that...so easily. I had Jeff to concentrate on so I never let myself feel and analyze it too much. If he'd had any feelings at all, he couldn't have just cut us off."

She looked genuinely upset, and Mac couldn't help but rest his hands on her shoulders and draw her closer. "Men like that aren't worth the heartache," he said bitterly. "My mother went through the same thing, and I still see the pain in her eyes the few times she's talked about my father. You've got to chalk up your marriage to a decision you made when you were too young to know better."

"But Jeff is the consequence of that decision, and I don't want him to pay for mistakes I made."

"What mistakes?"

"Maybe if I hadn't worked so many hours. Maybe if I'd given Robert what he needed..."

"Did you *know* what he needed?"

She shook her head. "And that in itself says a lot, doesn't it? I married to have the stable life I never had as a child. That was entirely the wrong reason. But I didn't realize it until it was too late."

Mac understood her regret. After the breakup of his engagement, he'd kicked himself up and down, wondering why he hadn't seen Maxine's true nature sooner, why he hadn't been more careful. He should have realized women saw his wealth and his lifestyle before they saw him. He didn't know if any woman had ever really known who he was as a man without all the trappings.

With Dina looking up at him, her eyes so relentlessly blue, her face so inescapably pretty, he couldn't resist satisfying the need that was growing much stronger than his hunger for food or his thirst for water. When he bowed his head, his body was screaming to have hers molded to his, to have her hands on his skin, and her arms around him. Visions of the pleasure they could share danced like illicit shadows all around them until her lips were soft under his, until his tongue parted her lips, until he was in the middle of the pleasure that could bring such keen satisfaction.

Dina's soft moan inflamed him further and he found himself passing his hands down her back, cupping her bottom, bringing her tight against him. For a few minutes they lived the desire that was enticingly wrapping around them. But then Dina's hands went to his chest and she shoved herself away.

"No," she said in a low voice. "This can't happen."

"Can't it?" he rasped. He wanted to see what she would do with this, where she would take it, what the next step in the dance was.

"Jeff and I will be moving on and I don't...I don't do one-night stands or...anything that could hurt my son." She looked so sincere standing there with her cheeks flushed, her lips pink from his kiss.

But she was making her position clear and he would, too. "And I'm not looking for anything more than that."

He didn't know if the startled look in her eyes was because he'd stated it flatly or maybe because she expected some confession or hope that this position wouldn't just be temporary.

"I guess men and women look at this kind of thing

differently.'' An awkward silence descended between them until she added, ''Thank you for getting Robert's number for me.'' Moving toward the door, she asked, ''What time would you like breakfast in the morning? I'll fix Jeff's around seven and take him to school afterward.''

''I have an early meeting tomorrow, so you don't have to make breakfast for me.''

She nodded, straightened her shoulders and murmured, ''Good night then.'' When she left his office, she closed his door.

Something had happened that Mac didn't like. Something that made him feel decidedly off balance. Although he knew getting involved with Dina would be a mistake, he didn't relish the idea of staying away from her, either.

When had this blue-eyed single mother gotten under his skin?

Keeping a distance from Dina wasn't that difficult, Mac thought, as he came home from work Monday evening. At least, it wasn't difficult in theory. Keeping her out of his head was a different matter. Last week had passed with them politely exchanging conversation whenever they ran into each other and at dinner. He and Jeff had played catch a couple of evenings before dark and their friendship was growing in leaps and bounds. However, Mac knew he had to keep some distance there, too.

So on Saturday he'd told Dina that her weekends were her own. Everyone deserved days off and that included her. He'd be spending all day Saturday at his office and going out Saturday night. It was a duty cocktail party, but he hadn't elaborated.

On Sunday though, he'd found himself wanting to hang around to be near both Dina and Jeff. Just knowing they were in his house filled his life somehow. It was odd. Sunday afternoon he and Jeff had stretched out in the family room watching a football game, and Dina had ended up making supper for all of them.

Going into the kitchen now, Mac found her taking baked potatoes from the oven. Jeff was telling her about a Christmas play at his school. As Mac stood listening, opening his tie, Jeff asked him, "Can you come and watch me, too?"

Dina said, "Mac's pretty busy."

Yes, he was, but this seemed to be important to Jeff. "You give me the time and date and I'll be there."

Dina gave him a surprised look. "I'll have dinner on the table in about ten minutes. Jeff, why don't you go wash up."

As Jeff scurried off to the bathroom, Mac asked, "Don't you want me to go to his play?"

"I just thought…I just thought you might not want to get too involved."

He deserved that, he supposed, and she was right. But he let her comment pass. "You still haven't heard from Craft?"

"No, and I'm so glad I didn't tell Jeff I was trying to reach him."

She sounded disappointed, and he wondered if it was for herself or for her son. She'd given Craft plenty of time to think about it. It was about time the man lived up to his responsibilities.

Mac said to her, "I have to make a phone call in my office. It shouldn't take more than ten minutes."

Wishing her pulse didn't race every time Mac got within ten feet of her, Dina watched him leave the kitchen. Their kiss the other night had swept her to a place where dreams mattered again, where second chances didn't seem to be as far away as the moon. But then Mac had brought her down to earth with a painful thump. He apparently didn't believe in commitment, long-term relationships, and especially not marriage. Not with her, at any rate. Chemistry was simply that…chemistry.

The trouble was—she had never felt chemistry as she felt it with Mac, and it seemed like so much more. But then, that was that little girl inside her, still trying to believe in the fairy tales her mother had once read to her.

She put dinner on the table and attempted appropriate comments during the meal, making sure she didn't look at Mac, making sure she would become immune to everything masculine about him. When they finished, he told her he had a meeting in Baltimore and wouldn't be back until late. That suited her just fine. The less she saw of him the better.

After she looked over Jeff's homework, they put puzzles together. As he got ready for bed, he said, "I like it here, Mom."

"We'll be moving as soon as I get another job," she warned. She didn't want him to get attached to anything about being here with Mac.

"Why can't you just keep this one?"

"Because I want more for me and I want more for you than just living here."

"You want to make dresses some day," he remembered.

She smiled at him. "Yes, I do."

When the phone rang, she gave him a kiss and hug good-night and then pulled his door almost shut. Hurrying to her bedroom, she picked up the phone. "Hello?"

"Call off your boyfriend."

"Who is this—? Robert?"

"I *figured* you wanted money."

"I don't know what you're talking about. I don't want any money. I want Jeff to know you."

"Sure, you do. That guy you sicced on me, Nightwalker something or other, said a man should know how to shoulder his responsibilities and that meant taking care of the children that belong to him in this world. Well, let me tell you, Dina, I'm not taking care of Jeff. I'm going to have a new wife and a new family and I don't want my old one interfering in that. So forget about me calling him. Forget about me, period. Got it?"

She couldn't believe this was the man she once loved. She couldn't believe he could be so callous. She also couldn't believe Mac had interfered in her business.

"Oh, I've got it, Robert. I'm sorry I even considered letting you back into Jeff's life. Now I know exactly what to tell him about you. You're a man who doesn't know how to be a husband or a father. He's better off with no father than one who doesn't know how to keep commitments."

When she slammed down the phone, tears came to her eyes and she tried to blink them away. Robert Craft wasn't worth her tears. He wasn't worth another thought. Yet she felt heartsick for Jeff just the same.

She tried to settle down and read through an issue of *Vogue* magazine. When she couldn't concentrate on that, she flipped on the TV. But nothing on there caught her attention, either. So she went out to the kitchen and made herself a cup of chamomile tea. Maybe that would calm her down. She'd baked apple muffins for breakfast and now she picked on one as she sipped at her tea, thinking back over her marriage...thinking back over her life.

She was just finishing her tea when she heard the garage door go up. Her pique at Mac for interfering in her life riled her all over again, and she knew she had to confront him about it. A few moments later, she heard the door open between the garage and the hallway that led past the laundry room into the kitchen.

When Mac appeared, he saw her sitting there and he stopped. "I thought you would have turned in."

He was so tall, so broad shouldered, so undeniably male that she pushed her chair back and stood so he wouldn't tower over her. But he still seemed to tower as she looked up at him. "What gave you the right to call my ex-husband and interfere in my life?"

Chapter Five

Mac knew he should table this discussion until morning. Dina was angry...he could tell from the silver sparks flashing in her eyes. She looked so damn beautiful. He was more inclined to take her into his arms and kiss her anger into passion than to discuss the phone call he'd made.

So much for the distance he'd been trying to put between them.

"Why? Why did you interfere?" she demanded to know again.

Annoyed that she saw his help as interference, he returned, "Because I thought your life could *use* some interference. Maybe then you could pay your phone bill *and* your heating bill."

For a moment she was speechless, and then her hurt look told him he had hit way below the belt. Yet after she took a deep breath, she continued to face him unwaveringly. "How many men do you know who would accept money from a woman who left them?"

"That's different," Mac insisted.

"Different? I don't think so. Sometimes pride is all a person has left," she said with a steadfastness that made him believe her pride was everything to her. "Robert walked out on me and Jeff," she went on. "He wouldn't even talk to me after he left, insisting his lawyer handle everything. Do you understand how that made me feel? He didn't want anything to do with us, and he made that perfectly clear. He didn't want to be a father or a husband. Why would I want to stay connected to a man like that?"

Thinking about his own childhood, he answered quickly, "For your son's sake."

She shook her head as her eyes still blazed at him. "I've handled my responsibilities toward my son just fine. When Robert and I were married, we were always in debt, and it wasn't just Jeff's medical bills. Robert charged whatever he wanted. He borrowed for whatever he needed, whether it was a car he thought he deserved or the new suit he wanted to wear to work. Since my divorce, I'm debt-free except for the medical bills I'm constantly paying. But that's all. I pay as I go, and I don't want any money from a man who doesn't want to give it."

"It's Jeff's due!"

Silence reverberated between them for a few heartbeats until she responded, "Maybe so. But there's an emotional cost to accepting money like that, and I don't want to pay it. I called Robert last week, not for money, but to see if he might want to be a father. All your call did was enrage him. I would have given him time to think over the whole situation, and maybe someday he would have called or written to his son.

Now he wants absolutely nothing to do with me or Jeff. Thanks to you.''

Mac hadn't looked at things from that perspective. He'd thought if Craft paid Dina child support, she wouldn't have to struggle to make ends meet. She wouldn't have to stay here…with him, distracting him, making him look at his life and analyzing what he saw. But it had backfired.

"Dina, I never meant—"

"You meant to do what *you* thought was best. But this is *my* life, Mac, and you had no right to control the path that I want to take. When you went out Saturday night, I didn't ask you where you were going or who you were going with. That's because I respect your privacy. I respect the fact that I'm working for you but have no right to make any judgments about your life. I expect you to afford me the same courtesy. Just because I'm taking a salary from you, doesn't give you the right to give me advice on how to run my life.''

With that, she turned away from him, went to the door that led down the small hall to her room and left him standing in the kitchen.

Mac drove his fingers through his hair, thinking about going after her. But he knew better than to do that.

He respected her for standing up to him. Not many people did. Dina Corcoran might look like a vulnerable young woman, but there was more to her than met the eye.

Restless and unsettled by his exchange with Dina, disconcerted by the amount of turmoil her presence and Jeff's in his life had caused, Mac knew he wouldn't get to sleep any time soon. Going up to his room, he quickly changed into his jogging suit and sneakers with reflectors. A good run might clear his head.

After resetting the security system, he went out the front door, stretched briefly, then began his run. He didn't have to worry about traffic this time of night. It seemed all of Hilldale closed its shutters and went to bed at least by ten.

As Mac ran, he heard Dina's voice clearly in his mind. *Just because I'm taking a salary from you, doesn't give you the right to give me advice on how to run my life.*

She'd been right. Why *had* he interfered?

Ever since he'd begun mentoring Jeff, unwanted thoughts about his own father had clicked through his head. All he knew about Frank Nightwalker was what his grandfather had told him. His mother never spoke about his dad, not freely anyway, and Mac had seen early on that his questions caused her pain. She'd always told him his father had left because the two of them weren't suited to each other. They were too different. Mac had accepted that, just as he'd accepted his grandfather's determination that Frank Nightwalker was a weak man who didn't know the value of family or tradition.

Was that true?

Mac raised his head to the late October wind. Maybe he'd interfered in Dina's life because he wished someone had interfered in his before he'd become an adult. He wished someone had called *his* father to tell him to think twice about shirking responsibilities, to live up to a commitment he'd made with marriage.

Commitment, vows, marriage—they didn't seem to mean very much to many people.

The cold night air brushed past Mac. His legs pumped harder as he increased his pace, as he tried to sort it all out.

It was an hour later when he approached the house again, more slowly, cooling down. After he automatically went through his after-run stretches, he let himself into the house, knowing what he had to do. Apologies didn't come easy to him. If he waited until morning, he might talk himself out of giving one to Dina.

Going down the hall to Dina's room, he was glad to see light under her door. He knocked softly.

When Dina came to the door, he noticed the lock didn't click when she opened it. Did that mean she felt safe in his house? Did that mean she trusted him?

When she saw him dressed in his running gear, she asked, "Is something wrong?"

She was wearing a long, pink and green flowered nightgown. It was soft flannel, and it concealed her from her neck to her ankles. But it also draped invitingly over her breasts, and Mac suddenly knew this was a very bad idea. He'd make this short and to the point and get back to his own room.

"Not in the way you mean. I just wanted to say—" The words seemed to stick to his tongue. "You were right. I shouldn't have interfered."

Her eyes widened a little, and she looked taken aback by his apology, such as it was. After a moment, she decided, "I shouldn't have said what I did. I'm sure your call to Robert didn't affect him one way or the other. It might have made him angry, but it wouldn't influence how he thought about Jeff." Then she admitted softly, "Sometimes my Irish temper gets the best of me. I overreacted."

The silent stillness of the night surrounded them as their gazes held and the memories of their kisses simmered in the space between them.

Finally Dina asked, "Did you call Robert only because you thought he should be paying me child support?"

She saw too much, and that bothered him almost as much as everything else about her. He could simply say yes and be done with it, but that wouldn't be the truth. "No, it wasn't only because of the child support. I called him because Jeff deserves a father, and he deserves to have his questions answered. I have questions about my own father. I wish someone had tapped him on the shoulder or hit him over the head with the responsibilities he walked away from."

"He never tried to contact you after he left?" Dina probed gently.

"My grandfather says he didn't. My mother won't talk about it. Suzette was only a year old, so none of it means very much to her. But I was three and my mind is shadowed with images of a tall man with a kind smile and gentle hands. It's just an impression, and maybe one I've made up."

Dina shook her head. "I doubt that. Children are very sensitive to everything that goes on around them, and I think they always carry the truth with them somewhere deep inside, even when they don't know they have it."

"I'd like to believe that's true," he said gruffly, looking down at her, wanting to kiss her again, even more now than he'd wanted to kiss her before. His body had started signaling to him exactly what it wanted as soon as she'd opened her door. But if he kissed her now, her bed was too close, and the truth was—he simply felt too damn vulnerable. Maybe it was the talk about his father, maybe it was the attraction to Dina he could no longer deny.

He took a step back then. "I'd better let you get to bed. I'll see you in the morning."

When she nodded, he turned and walked away, knowing a night's sleep wouldn't make him want her any less, knowing she'd become a fire in his blood, and he didn't know what he was going to do about it.

When Mac came home at lunchtime the following day, he went straight to his office for notes he'd forgotten on his desk that morning. He'd been awake most of the night with images of Dina in her nightgown flitting through his head. It wasn't like him to forget anything.

In his office, he picked up the manila folder and saw the invitation he'd inserted in the corner of the blotter. Fingering it, he opened it and studied it. It was another one of those social obligations he'd rather avoid, but sometimes at these bashes, he met up-and-coming talent Chambers' Enterprises could hire. The only problem was, he often had to fend off women batting their eyelashes at him. They always knew who he was. They always had a reason to want to talk to him, and it made doing real business damn difficult. If he took Dina along...

The thought both intrigued and unsettled him.

Birds chirped outside the long Palladian window and he gazed through the glass at the gardens, thinking about the lake beyond the woods. He'd been putting in a lot of hours. Dinner with Dina and Jeff and his exercise routine were his only breaks. Some time spent on the lake this afternoon might ease the restlessness inside of him and help him to relax. But first he should let Dina know he was here.

He hadn't heard her when he came into the house and now he wended his way to the kitchen. A low humming noise came from her bedroom, and he headed that way.

She was sitting at her small sewing machine, her back to him, with red-and-blue plaid material running under the needle. As she seriously concentrated on what she was doing, her hair fell forward softly along her cheeks, and he had the urge to run his fingers through it. He already knew it was silky. He already knew it smelled like spring.

When she took her foot off the pedal on the floor, he rapped on her door.

She jumped and looked over her shoulder. When she saw him, she smiled. "Hi. What are you doing home?"

"I forgot some papers this morning. What are you doing?"

Blushing, she said, "I hope you don't mind. I found curtain rods and fixtures in the closet, so I'm making valances for my room and Jeff's. I thought it would cozy them up a bit."

The double windows in both of their rooms were at the back of the house and were covered with wooden blinds.

She went on, "If you don't want me to leave them here when we move, I can take them along. I can use valances anywhere."

When he thought about her leaving, his chest tightened a little. It was odd. He knew as well as she did that this arrangement was only temporary. "You can do whatever you'd like with the rooms."

Remembering why he'd come to find her, he waved at the sunshine pouring through the blind. "I'm going to go out on the lake for a while." Then surprising himself, he asked, "Would you like to come with me?"

"What lake?" she asked, blinking at him.

"Lake Freemont borders the back of my property."

"Really? Isn't that the lake with the planned community all around it?"

"Yes, but I'm not part of that planned community. A natural reservoir of sorts extends along my back acreage. The developers left it as a channel and then enlarged it into the lake before I bought this property. I have a small boat dock. I've stored the Jet Ski for the season. But I keep a rowboat down there for fishing, until the lake freezes."

"You fish?" she asked, surprised.

"Are you telling me I don't look like a fisherman?" he joked.

Laughing, she shook her head. "My father's an avid fisherman when he's around water. I just don't put the two of you in the same category." After a pensive pause, she went on, "It would be nice to be out in the sun and air before winter really arrives. I can always finish these this evening. Did you eat lunch?"

"Not yet."

"Do you want me to pack a picnic?"

Her eagerness pleased him, and the afternoon took on an added dimension with her in it. "That'd be great. I'll go change and meet you in the kitchen."

Twenty minutes later as Mac and Dina walked through the woods, he wasn't entirely sure why he'd asked her to come along. He'd never minded being alone. As a youth he'd actually preferred it to lectures from his grandfather and classes at a private school. Being alone had always felt like a release. With no one else around, he could be himself.

Dina was carrying a blanket while he toted a round, insulated cooler. They didn't talk as they walked and listened to the sound of birds, the leaves rustling above them, the crunch of pine needles under their feet.

When they broke through the woods to the clearing and the dock, Dina said, "This is lovely!"

The sun struck the water with a brilliance that made it look like liquid light. Firs, willows dipping to the water and banks of laurel edged the channel at the back of his property.

Dina took a deep breath and absorbed it all. "You're so fortunate to have this in your backyard."

"I chose the property because of this. I could have found a house anywhere, but this..."

The sun not only glinted on the lake but on Dina's hair. He could see some red strands mixed with the blond and light brown. Her smile was almost as radiant as the day, and he felt a strange twisting in his gut. She looked so pretty in her pink sweater and jeans. The sun was warm on them and the breeze ruffled her hair now, teasing it across her cheek. It took everything in him to keep his hand by his side and not brush it away.

"Would you like to eat here on the dock or in the boat?" he asked.

"The boat."

The rowboat was tied to the dock. He dropped the cooler into it and then took the blanket from her, opening it onto the plank where she'd be sitting. After he helped her step in, he did, too. He pulled two life vests from a closed compartment and handed her one.

She put it on, then faced him, smiling. "I'm so glad you asked me to come along."

She looked like a child at an amusement park and he thought about how easy it was to make her happy. Or was it? Maybe her responses were more calculated than that. Maybe she was trying to get into his good graces and more into his life.

But he didn't want to entertain those suspicions today. He just wanted to enjoy himself and decided he was going to do that no matter what Dina was or was not trying to do. He rowed slowly for quite a while and they didn't talk, just enjoyed the sun, the blue sky, the green, gold, russet and oranges of nature around them. Eventually he rowed to the bank under the sweep of a willow so they'd have shade while they ate.

"Do you do this often?" she asked.

"Not often enough. More in the summer, though, when I have the Jet Ski out. Something about the speed of it helps me relax."

She laughed, a sweet musical sound that he found absolutely enchanting. "That sounds like a contradiction." She swept her arm over the lake. "But this…this would be heaven."

He unzipped the cooler, and she helped him take out the food and cans of soda. The boat rocked slightly, but she didn't seem bothered by it.

Handing him one of the sandwiches she'd made, she sat back with one of her own. "Do you hike much? Your woods are perfect for that, too."

"Sometimes on a Saturday afternoon, I pack my

backpack and take off into the hills. I've camped up there, too.''

"Alone?"

"Yes."

As she nibbled on her sandwich, he wondered if she wanted to know if he took women up there. Most women couldn't stand camping. They liked conveniences. But then, Dina hadn't had as many conveniences as the women he'd dated.

"What do you do when you go camping?" she asked curiously.

"Do?"

She nodded. "Some people birdwatch, others enjoy cooking over the campfire, some read by flashlight. What do you do?"

He thought about it and decided he went to the woods as some people might go to church, to get in touch with something more powerful than he was. "I soak it all in. Sometimes I wonder if liking it up there has something to do with my roots," he admitted.

"You mean being Cheyenne?"

"Yes. I guess that sounds foolish."

Shaking her head, she maintained, "That's not foolish at all. I think we carry with us everything our ancestors were, everything they felt and everything they did. I like the color green. Is it because I'm Irish? I like long grass and blue sky and dark beer, probably because of my dad, maybe because of *his* dad."

"Dark beer?" he repeated with a laugh.

She blushed. "I don't drink it often. I just like the taste. It's sort of like some folks taking their coffee black."

Her blue eyes danced at him, and he couldn't tell if she was pulling his leg or not. This was a playful side of her he hadn't seen before. He liked it, almost as much as her capacity for real passion. Unless she'd been pretending in his arms, unless she'd wanted him to think he was the only man who could awaken that kind of desire in her. Had she been that way with her husband?

"How did you meet your husband?" he asked her, more curious than he wanted to be about everything in her past.

She popped the last bit of her carrot stick into her mouth and didn't look disconcerted at his change of subject. "I was working at a tailoring shop then. Robert was the accountant who kept their books. I was only nineteen, he was twenty-two. I was so flattered when he took notice of me and asked me out. But I think I just wanted the stability marriage would give my life."

Was she seeking stability now? Security?

"Have you answered any more want ads?" He'd found her looking through the paper one night, circling phone numbers.

"There haven't been many to answer. I even called a new tailoring shop in Baltimore, but they've just hired a full-time seamstress. I might have to readjust my thinking about all of it. If I could take a few computer classes, I'd have another skill—word processing…something."

"I can teach you how to use the word processing program on my computer. There are several of them, but they're not all that different."

"That would be wonderful! Then I could practice my typing and get it up to speed again. I could manage with a secretarial job until I find a good seamstress position." She looked up at him almost shyly then.

"Eventually I want to take classes in fashion design. That's really what I've always wanted to do."

"I'm sure you will, then, if you're determined enough."

After she offered him a plastic bag filled with cookies, she checked her watch. "I guess we'd better start back. I have to pick up Jeff."

It was just as well they did start back. He was enjoying this afternoon too much, enjoying being with Dina too much.

After they repacked the cooler with their odds and ends and trash, Mac rowed back. At the dock, he tied the boat to the piling, then held it steady as Dina hopped out. He grabbed the cooler and blanket, and she took them from him.

After he stepped up onto the dock, they gazed at each other for a few moments. Then Dina said, "Thank you for asking me to join you."

When had he last spent an afternoon in a woman's company and really enjoyed it? The breeze ruffled Dina's hair against her cheek, and this time the temptation to brush it away was too strong to resist. His fingertips skimmed over the satin softness of her skin and then sank into the silkiness of her hair.

"Dina," he murmured, fighting desire that had a life of its own.

She seemed to have trouble fighting it too because her eyes became large and so blue they seemed to envelop him. His lips met hers with a demand that had been building all afternoon, maybe even since their last kiss. Under the sun, in the wake of the breeze, he held her to him, pressing their bodies together, invading her mouth with his tongue. Her arms went around his waist and she held on tightly, returning his passion with a hunger that matched his own. They were both still wearing the life jackets and the thickness kept them apart, kept them from feeling body against body, male against female, soft against hard.

His body cried out for satisfaction and he broke the kiss to mutter, "Damn life jackets." He tore open the Velcro tabs and ridded himself of his.

Dina just stood there, her fingers going to the fastening, but then not pulling it open.

He did it for her and brushed the jacket from her shoulders until it landed on the dock.

Looking up at him, she said, "Mac, I'm not sure we should—"

But at that moment, he didn't want to hear about "shoulds," he didn't want to hear his grandfather's voice telling him what kind of woman he should or shouldn't get involved with. He didn't want to think about what came afterward. Holding her face between his hands, he just wanted to taste her sweetness and fulfill the need that pulsed through him like quicksilver.

This time when he enfolded her in his arms, his hand covered her breast and she moaned under his caress. He thought about laying her down right there on the dock and taking her. Just the idea made him wonder what had come over him, what kind of spell she'd woven about him.

Tearing his mouth from hers, he looked down at her and tried to control his breathing. Not too fast, he warned himself. Go slow with this if you're going to go at all. Bide your time and put one foot in front of the other very carefully.

Somehow logic slowed his racing blood and he reluctantly released her. "You'll be late getting Jeff," he said.

"Yes, I will." Her voice was as thready and breathless as he felt.

Turning away from her, he picked up the cooler and the blanket, but when he straightened, he'd made a decision. "There's a party Saturday night that I have to attend. Would you like to go with me?"

Chapter Six

On Saturday evening as Dina looked into the mirror and applied lipstick, she knew she should have refused Mac's invitation to this party. But she hadn't been able to resist the chance to spend more time with him and maybe even feel like Cinderella for a night. She'd asked herself over and over again why he had invited *her* when he could practically have his pick of any date in the country. Yet after that last kiss, she'd hoped he simply wanted to be with her as she wanted to be with him.

Still, warning bells were going off in her head. *You should know better. You've got to think of Jeff. You've got to protect your heart.*

"I *am* going to protect my heart," she said to her reflection in the mirror. "This is one date, one night. I'm just going to have fun."

Trudy MaGuinnis, the neighbor from Dina's old apartment building who had watched Jeff after school, had been thrilled with the idea of baby-sitting at Mac

Nightwalker's house. Because she preferred not to drive at night, Mac had offered to pick her up.

Dina would have liked nothing better than to go shopping and splurge on an expensive dress for tonight, but she had her future and her son's to think about, and she wanted to add as much as she could to her nest egg. It had been so long since she'd gotten dressed up that she'd almost forgotten she had this dress in her closet. It was royal blue crepe. She'd designed and sewn it herself for a party she'd attended with Robert when they were married. The halter top was sedate in the front but cut low in the back. The skirt gathered around her slim waist and fell well above her knees.

Thank goodness that length was fashionable again. High-heeled black suede pumps and a matching purse completed the outfit. She'd managed to swirl her hair into a French twist, leaving a few stray waves to dangle around her face. Fortunately the black wool coat she'd bought a few years ago was a classic style. She hoped Mac would be proud of the way she looked, that she could hold her own in his crowd. For a final touch she'd added pearl drop earrings to her ears, hoping no one could tell they weren't real.

Taking from her drawer a small bottle of perfume that a co-worker had given her one Christmas, she dabbed some behind her ears, at the pulse point of her throat and on her wrists. She usually didn't wear perfume because of Jeff's asthma—some scents made him react and others didn't—but tonight she wouldn't be around him very much. And if Mac got close at all...

Jeff's footsteps sounded in the hall as he ran toward her room and announced, "They're here."

Her heart beat faster as she picked up her coat and took it to the kitchen. When Trudy MaGuinnis saw Dina, she smiled and then gave her a huge hug. Dina hugged her back. She'd missed her. Trudy was sixty-five, with frizzy gray hair and sparkling brown eyes. She lived on her husband's pension and Social Security benefits and was always willing to help out Dina when needed. With Christmas two months away, Dina knew the older woman could use the baby-sitting money she would pay her tonight for Christmas presents for her grandchildren.

Abruptly Trudy pushed away and held Dina at arm's length. "My, don't you look pretty!"

"Thank you," Dina said with a laugh. "Is Mac waiting in the car?" She didn't hear him or see him.

"Oh, no. He escorted me in, but then he pointed me in here and said he had to pick up some business cards in his office."

Jeff took the older woman's hand. "Come with me, Mrs. MaGuinnis. I want to show you my room."

After Trudy exclaimed over Jeff's new digs and Dina gave her a list of emergency phone numbers, they walked toward the kitchen.

Trudy said, "You sure are coming up in the world. Imagine you living here with Mac Nightwalker. Who would have thought. If fortune smiles down on you, maybe this will become more than a job."

Before Dina could form a protest, she heard Mac's footfalls as he appeared in the kitchen doorway. She hoped he hadn't heard Trudy's comment.

His expression was unreadable as his gaze passed over her, from her dangling earrings to her high-heeled pumps. His eyes turned almost black, as they had before he kissed her, but he didn't comment on her appearance.

Instead, he said, "I'm ready whenever you are."

"I'm ready," she assured him, hoping it was true.

The inside of Mac's car was sumptuous with its sleek black leather and burled walnut. But as the silence grew long between them during the drive, Dina wasn't as comfortable as she should have been.

"Do you work with Calvin Reynolds?" she asked, hoping to start a conversation. Mac had told her Calvin Reynolds and his wife were throwing the party. She'd put the man's name and phone number on the emergency list with the others after Mac had given it to her.

"Not exactly."

"They're friends?"

"More or less."

His terse comment made her wonder again if he'd overheard Trudy's remark. Did he think she'd taken the job with him...to what? Entice him to support her? More?

She couldn't ask him if he'd overheard. It would be too embarrassing. Besides, she wasn't altogether sure of her reasons for accepting his job, although she'd convinced herself she'd taken it for Jeff's sake. Maybe the idea of being around Mac had been too tempting to resist, though she'd denied it at the time. Since their afternoon on the lake, she was feeling entirely too giddy over their kiss...feeling entirely too much for him.

A short while later, she tried again to make conversation. But Mac's monosyllabic response didn't encourage her and she soon gave up.

When they reached the house where the party was

located, Mac came around to her side of the car and
helped her out, then handed his keys to a valet. The
contemporary-styled glass and cedar house was huge.

As soon as the maid led them to a large open living
room, Mac introduced her to Calvin and Marcia Reynolds. The couple looked to be in their thirties. Dina
could tell her hostess was giving her the once-over,
but when they spoke for a few moments she was
friendly.

Soon after, Mac led Dina to the bar. "Would you
like something to drink?"

As she covertly studied the other guests, she murmured, "White wine would be great."

When Mac handed her the stemmed glass, his fingers brushed hers and she gazed up into his eyes. But
what she saw there, or rather didn't see there, concerned her. She thought they'd come to have a good
time. But Mac's stance was stiff, his expression removed. It was as if he'd shut her out. Maybe she
should have brought up Trudy's remark, embarrassing
or not.

"If you don't mind, I need to mingle," he said, his
voice almost that of a stranger. "There are a few people I came to meet."

"I don't mind. I can wander over to the hors
d'oeuvres table—"

"No, I'd like you to come with me."

She suspected Mac wanted to initiate informal conversation with other couples. Maybe he could get to
know people better that way. "Sure," she agreed.

She was quiet at first as they mingled, just looking
and listening, getting a feel for the people who were
there, not wanting to say anything that would be a gaff
Mac would regret. When one gentleman offered his

The Silhouette Reader Service™ — Here's how it works:

NO POSTAGE
NECESSARY
IF MAILED
IN THE
UNITED STATES

BUSINESS REPLY MAIL
FIRST-CLASS MAIL   PERMIT NO. 717   BUFFALO, NY

POSTAGE WILL BE PAID BY ADDRESSEE

SILHOUETTE READER SERVICE
3010 WALDEN AVE
PO BOX 1867
BUFFALO NY 14240-9952

Play The Lucky Hearts Game

and get...
FREE BOOKS & a FREE GIFT...
YOURS to KEEP!

Yes! I have scratched off the silver card. Please send me my **2 FREE BOOKS** and **FREE MYSTERY GIFT**. I understand that I am under no obligation to purchase any books as explained on the back of this card.

Scratch Here!
then look below to see what your cards get you...

opinion on the public school system in Hilldale, Dina joined in on the discussion since she was familiar with programs added this year and the teachers in the district.

After the conversation came to a natural end, Mac bent low to her ear and asked, "Would you like something to eat?"

His breath on her cheek made her heart race, and she nodded.

While he was gone, she noticed two women standing by the bar, eyeing her curiously. One made a comment and the other frowned. Dina didn't like being the object of their speculation.

Mac returned to her and they seated themselves on a love seat, sampling the buffet. Dina had the feeling that eyes were on her again. A redhead about her own age stood by a set of bookshelves and glanced at her every so often. It made Dina uncomfortable. Mac was speaking to the man beside him about real estate development, and the two women on the other side of their small circle were discussing funding for an art show. Dina had never been more aware that she didn't belong here.

Sliding her dish to the coffee table and standing, she said to Mac, "I'm going to powder my nose."

After a nod of acknowledgment that he'd heard her, she made her way through the living room and the parlor to a hallway leading to the bathroom. She took her time, patting a few curls into place, making sure her nose wasn't shiny, reapplying lipstick. But the truth was, she was stalling. She didn't want to go back out there. Yes, she liked being with Mac, and everyone had been polite. But she felt that this was a closed circle, one where she didn't belong. There was talk of investments and portfolios and whether the price of gold would drop or rise. She knew nothing about foundations or charity work, at least not the type these women discussed. She was more familiar with thrift shops and soup kitchens where she'd volunteered now and then. She'd thought tonight would be fun and she would feel like Cinderella. But she didn't. She simply felt out of place.

When she exited the powder room, a tall blonde stood there waiting, one of the two women who had been positioned at the bar earlier, watching her.

Dina smiled at her. "Sorry I took so long. I didn't know anyone was waiting."

The blonde returned her smile, but Dina could tell it wasn't genuine. It looked much too practiced. "I just needed a breather from the chitchat. You're with Mac Nightwalker, aren't you?"

Dina nodded.

"Have you been dating long?"

Panicking for a moment, Dina didn't know how to respond. But then she said simply, "Mac and I are friends."

The blond woman, whose beaded dress probably cost as much as Dina could make in a month, gave her a sly smile. "Such a diplomatic answer. There are a few women here who wouldn't mind being 'friends' with Mac."

Dina was embarrassed by the insinuation as well as the questioning and felt her temper bristle. "I didn't catch your name," she said pleasantly, though she was feeling anything but pleasant.

"It's Lois. Lois Myers. And yours was...Dana?"

"Dina."

Still obviously fishing for information, Lois offered,

"Maybe I'll see you at the symphony with Mac next week."

Unable to resist, Dina answered, "Mac and I haven't checked our calendars yet to see if the symphony will fit into our schedule." Then before she could get into real trouble, she excused herself and returned to the living room.

The redhead Dina had seen glancing at her earlier was sitting beside Mac now on the love seat, her hand on his arm. Dina felt a pang of jealousy she had no right to feel.

When Mac saw her, he stood, excused himself from the group, and came toward her. "If you're ready to leave, I'll get your coat."

The redhead still looked up at him with hungry eyes. There were women here tonight with and without escorts who had watched him move from group to group. Dina was all too aware of the envious stares. It had taken all evening, but she finally realized why he'd invited her along tonight. She didn't like the reason any one bit.

She nodded that she, too, was ready to leave. In fact, the sooner, the better.

Once in the car she was as silent as he had been during the drive to the party. She felt him glance at her every once in a while, but she kept her gaze straight ahead, feeling hurt and used. She'd thought Mac had asked her along tonight because he liked her company, because he wanted to be with her, because of the chemistry that sizzled between them. But now she realized she'd deluded herself.

Finally Mac turned into the driveway to his house. "I'll just park in front if you don't mind going in and getting Trudy."

"That's fine," she said curtly.

She felt his gaze on her again, but he didn't say anything as he veered around the circle to the front of the house. Then before she could hop out, he switched off the ignition and asked, "Is something wrong, Dina?"

She counted a few beats of her pulse before she decided to tell him exactly what was troubling her. "Yes, something's wrong. I finally figured out why you asked me to go with you tonight."

The yellow light illuminating the front door glowed over them. Mac's brows drew together as he asked, "And what conclusion did you come to?"

"You wanted a buffer. You wanted someone safe who would act as your date and keep other women at bay."

He let out a sigh. "I needed to mingle for business purposes, not get caught up in conversations with women who were interested in a date for the symphony."

"Or a night in your bed?" Dina asked with some heat. Those women didn't want a date to the symphony. They wanted to be with Mac—the man, in his bed, in his arms. Dina knew it was true, because part of her longed for that, too.

"Is that what *you* want?" he asked finally. "Or maybe even more?"

Mac's composure ruffled her as much as Lois's had, but this time she didn't hold her feelings in. Apparently he *had* heard Trudy's remark and she needed to address it. "I went along tonight because I thought it would be fun. And I took your job because I need to save enough money to get my own place and find work that will support Jeff and me. Apparently you'd rather believe I have some other motive. Well, you believe what you want. Thanks for the evening, Mr. Nightwalker, but I don't think I'll be trying that particular type of date again. It wasn't much fun.''

Quickly she opened the car door and climbed out. Then she practically ran into the house, tears burning in her eyes. At least Robert had never made her feel as if she weren't good enough for him. At least Robert had never used her as Mac just had.

But as she hurried to the kitchen, she knew she'd never quite felt about Robert the way she felt about Mac. That scared her as much as the possibility that she wouldn't find work so she and Jeff could be independent again.

Mac had come to his den on his return to the house, reminding himself his desire for Dina could be ignored. During the past two weeks, he'd congratulated himself on keeping his life separate from hers. He'd made certain he'd left before breakfast and come home late. Once in a while they'd shared dinners, though since the night of the cocktail party any conversation had been strained. This past weekend, Dina had taken Jeff to Baltimore to the zoo, and Jeff had asked Mac if he wanted to go along. But Mac had declined, aware that the boy was disappointed.

It was simply better not to get too involved, better not to let Jeff get too attached. Trudy MaGuinnis's remark to Dina the night they'd gone out still rankled. *If fortune smiles down on you, maybe this will become more than a job.* Dina had looked devastatingly hurt when he'd tossed his accusations at her, but that could have been an act.

Though he was still lost in thought, Mac came instantly alert when he heard a tentative rap on the door.

Jeff opened the door, and Mac smiled at him. "What's up, sport?"

"I need your help," the seven-year-old said.

All of Mac's focus was instantly trained on Jeff. "What kind of help?"

Approaching uncertainly, Jeff placed a piece of paper in front of Mac. "I want to play soccer. If you put your name on that, I can."

Mac picked up the form and read it. It was a permission slip for a parent to sign, allowing his or her child to play indoor soccer. "I can't sign this, Jeff. I don't have the authority. Your mom has to sign it."

Jeff looked up at him with the same wide blue eyes as Dina's, and his lower lip trembled. "Mom won't sign. She's afraid I'll have another attack. I promised her I won't, but she won't believe me."

Standing, Mac came around the desk and leaned against it, placing his hand on Jeff's shoulder. "I don't think you can make that kind of a promise, can you?"

Tears came to Jeff's eyes. "I won't forget to take my medicine and use my inhaler again, so I won't get an attack. It only happened the last time because I forgot. And then I'd told Mom I'd used it when I hadn't. I get tired of taking medicine. But I will, honest, if I can play soccer."

Mac realized how the asthma made Jeff feel different. Yet he also remembered the expression on Dina's face as she'd watched her son turn blue. "Your mom has to decide what's best for you, sport. I can't do that."

"But I want to play like everybody else. It's not fair!"

Old enough to know life wasn't fair, Mac didn't argue the point. On the other hand, he could see Jeff really wanted to do this, and that he was terribly upset by Dina's decision not to let him. "I'll tell you what. I can't sign your form, but I can talk to your mom."

"Right now?" Jeff pleaded.

"Sure, I can do it now. Why don't you go watch TV."

"Mom's emptying the dishwasher," Jeff said helpfully.

Mac smiled. "Okay, I'll see what I can do."

Dina was indeed emptying the dishwasher. She stood on tiptoe, trying to put a serving dish in one of the upper cupboards. Moving toward her quickly, Mac reached above her, took the dish from her fingers and placed it on the shelf. He was close enough to her that if he dropped his chin a notch, it would be in her hair. Her bottom was against his thighs, and he was hard in an instant.

"Thank you," she murmured.

He backed away from her, frustrated with himself because he wanted to be around her, talk to her, kiss her. "I never did understand why they put shelves so high that women can't reach them," he muttered.

Her cheeks were flushed, and she laughed. "I know what you mean."

There was an awkward silence as neither of them seemed to know what to say, and he remembered why he had come to the kitchen. "Jeff knocked on my door a few minutes ago."

"Did he bother you?"

"No. Actually he wanted my help with something."

She looked puzzled. "Homework? He told me he had it all finished."

"Not homework." Mac handed her the permission slip he'd folded into his left hand. "He wanted me to sign this."

Apparently she knew what it was without even looking at it. "I'm sorry. I said no and I guess he thought—"

"That you were being unreasonable."

That brought her eyes back to his. "How can you say that…?"

"*I'm* not saying it. That's what he thought. I know how scared you were after what happened at the park."

She studied him for a few moments. "But you do think I'm being unreasonable."

"I only know what Jeff told me. He said he promised you he'd use his inhaler and he promised you he wouldn't have another attack. Now I know he can't do that. But aren't there precautions you can take so he could play on the team?"

"Are you interfering again?" she asked succinctly.

"*Your* son came to *me*. This wasn't any of my business until he pulled me into it. When I told him I didn't have the authority to sign this permission slip, he looked devastated. So I came up with another option. I told him I'd talk to you."

"All right. You've talked to me, and my answer is still no. You have no idea what it's like to see your son struggling for breath, to see his lips turning blue."

Mac could only imagine the heartache of a mother feeling powerless to help her child. Still… "When are you going to start taking Jeff's feelings and wishes into account? When is he going to be old enough to have a say in what he does?"

"When I decide he's old enough."

"By then, you might have trained him to be so cautious, he won't try anything new."

Altogether impatient with him now, she said resolutely, "Look, Mac, I'm raising my son the way I see fit. I'll talk to him about this again and explain—"

"Explain you won't let him enjoy life like other kids because you're afraid he's going to suffer?"

She threw up her hands in frustration. "You know nothing about asthma!"

"I know what I've read about athletes who have asthma, and they still compete. Is Jeff such a special case that he can't do that?"

His question hung in the kitchen, almost vibrating the cabinets, but Dina didn't answer. She turned around to the dishwasher, took two plates from it, opened the cupboard, and settled them inside with a bit of noise.

"Not only do you have an Irish temper, but you're stubborn," Mac decided.

She ignored him, and that made him angry.

"All right. I've said my piece," he said to her back. "But the least you can do is call Jeff's doctor and talk to him about it. Show your son that you're flexible enough to get someone else's advice."

After Dina took Jeff to school the following morning, she called his doctor. In spite of the tension between her and Mac, as well as the lingering hurt that made her want to dismiss what he said, she'd decided he was right. As Jeff became older, he deserved to have a say in what he did and didn't do. He'd told her he'd used his inhaler before they'd gone to the park, but he hadn't. He'd gotten tired of the routine of it, like kids do. Still, he had to learn to take responsibility for his asthma since he'd be living with it for the rest of his life. She had to put her fear aside to figure out what was best for him.

She talked to Dr. Mansfeld at length about Jeff playing sports. The doctor had told her before that Jeff needed exercise as much as he needed to learn his limits, and he reminded her of that again. Dina expressed all of her concerns and the doctor addressed each of them. The bottom line was, along with taking precautions and educating the coach on Jeff's condition, she should let him play.

Later that day after she'd brought Jeff home from school and told him, he was ecstatic and gave her a huge hug that brought tears to her eyes. He wanted to tell Mac, of course, but bedtime arrived before Mac came home.

It was nine-thirty when Dina heard the garage door open. She decided to give Mac time to change clothes and get comfortable. The truth was, she still felt raw about the night he'd taken her to the Reynolds' party. Admitting he'd been right about allowing Jeff to play soccer wouldn't be easy.

After a half hour or so, Dina went looking for him, thinking she'd find him in the family room or his den. But both rooms were dark. She went to the foot of the stairs and listened, but no sound came from the second floor. Listening more closely, she realized she could hear music. Following the vibrations of it, she opened the door to the basement and found the lights ablaze. Descending the stairs, passing by the Ping-Pong and pool tables, she headed toward the music and the workout room. She stopped in the doorway when she saw him working out on the Nautilus.

Wearing a T-shirt and running shorts, Mac creased

his brow in concentration as he pulled a weighted bar up and down. His T-shirt was wet with perspiration, and the muscles in his arms flexed as he exerted himself. His stomach was flat, and the sight of his hair-roughened legs gave her a curling sensation in her tummy. He was a wonderfully built male and she'd never been so attracted to anyone in her life.

After their "date," when she realized that he had the power to hurt her, she'd had to admit to herself she was falling in love with him. But she had to stop herself from tumbling further into a deep ravine that would only bring her heartache.

When she moved into the room, he must have seen her from the corner of his eye. He let the weights clang to a stop. She spotted her reflection in the mirrored wall to his left, and she wished she'd applied a touch of lipstick before she'd come looking for him.

Swiping a towel from the silver bar beside him, he wiped his face with it and switched off the music. "I thought you'd turned in."

"Not yet. I...I wanted to talk to you first."

He hung his towel around his neck and waited.

"I called Jeff's doctor. After talking to him, I decided to let Jeff play soccer."

"I'll bet he's pleased," Mac commented, his expression unreadable.

"More than pleased. I just wanted to tell you that you were right that I should put my fears aside and do what is best for him. His doctor made me see that. I'm not used to taking anybody else's advice where Jeff is concerned. I had to make all the decisions about his welfare even when I was married. I guess that's why I balked when you expressed your opinion."

Mac's dark eyes were intent on hers. "I'm not as

close to the situation as you are, so I guess my perspective is just a little broader.''

Standing so close to Mac like this, inhaling his male scent, almost feeling the heat of his skin, she realized how powerfully virile he was. But he was out-of-bounds for her and he had proved that.

She tore her gaze from his, murmuring, ''That's all I wanted.''

But when she turned to go, he caught her by her shoulder. ''Dina.''

When he said her name, something in his voice made her turn to look at him again.

''The party at the Reynolds'…'' he began.

She knew all of the hurt she felt that night was in her eyes. Shaking her head, she tried to pull away.

But he wouldn't let her. ''I had more than one reason for asking you to go with me,'' he insisted. ''It's true I knew you would be a buffer. But I also asked you along because I wanted to be with you. I knew you would make the evening more pleasant.''

Had the past two weeks of distance between them been as difficult for him as they had been for her? ''Really?'' she asked, afraid to hope he *did* care for her.

As he studied her, he slowly nodded. ''Really.'' Then he pulled her closer, reached out and brushed her hair back behind her ear. ''You were the most beautiful woman there.''

His voice was husky, his gaze brimming with the desire she'd glimpsed before. Blushing, she didn't know what to say.

Finally he cleared his throat. ''Thanksgiving is next week. Do you and Jeff have any plans?''

"No. I sent my father this address and phone number, but I haven't heard from him."

A few moments passed and it seemed as if Mac was turning something over in his mind. Then he asked, "How would you like to come to Oak Hill with me?"

"Oak Hill?"

"That's the name of my grandfather's estate. I'll tell them I'm bringing two guests."

"You're sure your family won't mind?"

He shook his head. "They won't mind. The only thing is... I'd rather not tell them you're my housekeeper. There would be too many questions. I'll simply tell them that I've been mentoring Jeff through the Y and that we're friends."

She could understand Mac not wanting his family prying into his life. "Are we friends?" she asked.

After he searched her face, he answered, "I think we're getting there." Then he dropped his hands and stepped away from her, hanging his towel back over the bar. "Think about whether or not you'd like to go. Jeff might enjoy seeing the horses in the stables."

It would be nice not to spend Thanksgiving alone this year. Jeff would like being with Mac. She would, too. She suspected this was Mac's way of making up for the night of the party.

Weighing the pros and cons of his invitation, deciding she'd like to meet his family because then she might understand Mac better, she said, "We'd like to spend Thanksgiving with you."

His gaze seemed to consume her for a few moments. "I'll let my mother know you and Jeff will be coming." Then he repositioned himself at the bar, obviously intent in getting on with his exercise regimen.

Dina murmured good-night, the feel of his hand in

her hair still a lingering sensation that made her tingle, the piercing intensity of his gaze still burning her soul.

Although Joseph Chambers was in his seventies, he had a vigor about him that belied his years. His blond hair was laced with gray, but his blue eyes were sharp. He turned them on Dina now as he ate the last bite of turkey on his plate. "Mac has never brought a guest for Thanksgiving dinner before."

It was a statement with an implied question. Up until now, Joseph Chambers, Mac's mother Leona and his sister Suzette had engaged in nonthreatening conversation that Dina could either join in on or not as she felt inclined.

"I was pleased Mac invited us. If I'd made a turkey for me and Jeff, we'd be eating it for a week," she responded with a smile.

"You don't have family in the area?" Leona Chambers asked. There was a haughtiness about Leona that Dina suspected originated from having servants and living a life of having every need gratified.

"No, we don't have family in the area," she answered easily.

"But you do have family?" Leona persisted. She too was ash-blond. Her hair was curled and arranged around her face to perfection. She was a feminine version of her father.

"My mother's deceased, but my father's in Florida."

After a sip of water, Mac's sister, Suzette, set down her glass and also set her gaze on Dina. Unlike her mother, Suzette had dark brown hair and brown eyes, but her facial features also resembled her grandfather's. Only Mac looked Cheyenne. "I understand you accompanied my brother to the Reynolds' party a few weeks ago,'' she remarked offhandedly.

At this point, Mac intervened. ''Is one of your friends gossiping about me again?'' he asked with a playful note, deflecting the attention away from Dina.

''I spoke with Lois. She mentioned you were there with someone new.''

New? Dina wondered. She supposed that meant someone who was unknown to Mac's usual circle of friends.

Dina noticed Leona offering Jeff the dish of cranberry salad. Mac's mother smiled at him differently than she smiled at everyone else. There was a softness there. It told Dina she liked children.

As the maid cleared the dinner plates, Jeff tugged on Dina's arm. ''Did you see the pool over there, Mom?''

Jeff had been in awe of the mansion with its many wings ever since they'd arrived. Oak Hill was situated atop a wooded hill about an hour from Hilldale, on the outskirts of northern Baltimore. The setting, as well as the house, looked like something out of a movie. Through the dining room windows, they could see the indoor pool from where they were sitting.

''Yes, I did see the pool. Maybe we could get a closer look after dinner.''

Leona's hand fingered the pearls at her neck. ''You don't have to just look. You can try it out.''

''Can we, Mom?'' Jeff asked excitedly.

''We don't have our suits,'' she said practically.

''Oh, that's no problem,'' Suzette remarked. ''We keep extra suits for guests. I'm sure we can find something.''

''Matter of fact,'' Leona went on, ''why don't you

stay the night? That would give you the opportunity to go riding tomorrow if you'd like.''

Dina swallowed hard.

Jeff was practically hopping out of his seat. ''Can we, Mom? Can we? I've never ridden a horse.''

Dina's gaze met Mac's now. It wasn't really up to her.

''Would you like to stay?'' he asked her quietly.

''Oh please, please, Mom. Can we?'' Jeff asked again.

''We don't even have our toothbrushes,'' she joked.

''We have fresh ones in each guest bedroom,'' Leona assured her. ''And you and Suzette look to be about the same size. She probably has a nightgown you can borrow.''

This was a wonderful adventure for Jeff as well as for her. She'd never been in surroundings that were so sumptuous, elegant, extravagant—from the crystal chandeliers to the damask and tapestries. She supposed it wouldn't hurt to spend the night. She'd spoken to Jeff about not saying anything concerning their stay at Mac's house. She'd told him it was their secret for now, and her son had agreed to keep it. But she felt as if she was deceiving Mac's family, and she didn't like it. Still, Mac had explained again that he didn't want to answer a lot of questions and it would be simpler not to go into details.

Searching Mac's face, but unable to read his thoughts, she responded to Leona, ''I think my son would be very disappointed if I said no. We'd be glad to accept your hospitality for the night.''

''After we finish here,'' Leona said, ''I'll show you and Jeff around the stables.'' She winked at the seven-year-old. ''I have the perfect horse for you to ride.''

"I was going to show them around, Mother," Mac said, brows furrowed.

"I'd like to get to know Dina and Jeff better. I'm sure you can find something to occupy yourself for a little while."

The maid brought in a serving tray with slices of pumpkin pie topped with whipped cream. As she set one in front of Dina, Dina knew she'd better put on her tap dancing shoes. Leona Chambers was going to give her the third degree and she'd better be prepared.

Chapter Seven

When Mac found the small cedar box in a cabinet in the attic, there were two photo albums lying underneath it that he'd never seen before. With Dina and Jeff at the stables with his mother, he'd been drawn up here for the first time in years. The situation with Jeff and Robert Craft had stirred up questions in Mac about his own father, and now he wanted some answers.

Taking the albums out of the cabinet with the box, he sat on the floor with all of it. The white album was obviously a wedding album. He opened it, and his chest tightened.

There was a picture of his mother in a satin gown and long veil, looking into the eyes of the man Mac recognized as his father. There was no doubt about Mac's resemblance to him. As he studied the couple in the photo, Mac saw that they looked totally absorbed in each other. Turning picture after posed picture, he could feel happiness radiating from them. His father looked like a tall, strong man who had wanted nothing more than to spend his life with the woman he had taken as his wife.

What had happened?

The second album contained pictures of Mac's first two years. He wasn't interested in himself as a child. Rather, he studied the faces of the two people who should have meant the most to him in the whole world. But as he flipped page after page, he saw his father's expression become more serious. Month after month, something changed. The smile Frank Nightwalker gave the camera wasn't genuine and when he looked at Mac's mother, there seemed to be longing there. What had happened to the happiness?

The last photo in the album was of Suzette's christening. Mac's grandfather held her as Frank and Leona looked on, Mac by their side. Frank's expression was troubled.

Had a second child brought more parental responsibility than his father had wanted to shoulder? Was that why he had left?

Setting the albums aside, Mac opened the box. There he found mementos he'd looked through as a child, not understanding what they were. There was a woman's hair comb inlaid with turquoise and agate. Had it been a present to his mother from his father? In a small blue box atop a piece of cotton, he found two rings. Both were bands inlaid with turquoise and onyx, carnelian and lapis. The mosaic was the same on both, and they looked like wedding bands.

Picking up the album again, he searched for pictures of his parents' hands. His father wore the mosaic band. But on his mother's finger, he found a diamond wed-

ding ring. Another part of the puzzle that didn't make
any sense.

Also in the box, Mac found a small piece of pottery,
a two-spouted wedding vase, as well as a leather wrist
band with Leona's name spelled in beads. The last
item was a suede, fringed pouch. When Mac opened
it, he spilled three arrowheads into his hand. He ran
his thumb over them, not knowing what they meant,
either. Why had his mother kept them? Why had his
mother kept any of this?

He put it all away, wondering why he wanted to stir
up the past, why any of it should mean anything. He
was an adult. He knew who he was. He was living his
life the way he wanted it. Whoever his father had been
didn't matter any more.

But as Mac descended the steps from the attic, he
felt restless and off balance and in need of a good
swim to work off excess energy.

Dina pulled open the glass door to the indoor swimming pool and stepped inside. It was dark outside the
many plate glass windows. Underwater lights illumi-
nated the pool, and one table lamp lit the area by the
chaise lounge. As humidity wrapped around her, the
blue-green ambiance of the ceramic tile as well as the
pool liner made the room seem an other-worldly place.

Leona had not only given her and Jeff a tour of the
stables, but a tour of the whole estate. When she'd
asked if Dina worked, Dina had told her she was in
the fashion industry. She didn't like stretching the
truth, but it wasn't a lie, either. Strangely, Leona
hadn't asked any other questions. She'd been very
friendly to Jeff, and he'd chattered on to her about
everything and anything he saw. She'd introduced him

to the cook, and he was in the kitchen now having a snack. Dina had told Jeff they could swim before he went to bed, but she'd come in search of Mac because she hadn't seen him for the past two hours and wondered what he was up to.

Now she found him swimming laps. As she watched, she saw that he was swimming as if the devil were chasing after him. His long strong arms cut sharply into the water as his legs scissored, propelling him forward. When he came to the edge of the pool, he flipped underwater to make a return trip. He was totally oblivious to everything except what he was doing.

Mesmerized, Dina watched him for ten more laps, thinking she should stop him, thinking he was working himself much too hard.

Suddenly instead of a flip underwater, he came up for air in the shallow end and ran his hands back over his hair.

"Mac?" she asked softly.

Turning, he saw her. He didn't say anything, just hoisted himself over the edge, grabbed a white towel that was lying on the tiles, and slung it around his shoulders. Water glistened on his body and she couldn't help staring, taking in his smooth chest, his taut stomach, his sleek black swimsuit and everything it detailed, his long legs. Her stomach somersaulted and she felt a bit breathless.

He walked toward her, his expression sober. "How long have you been here?"

"Long enough to see you swim with a vengeance. Is something wrong?"

He didn't answer her right away but rather toweled

off his hair, then slung the terry cloth around his neck. "I found something in the attic—" He stopped.

She'd never seen Mac look this troubled and waited for him to say more.

Finally he gazed at her steadily. "When you look at me, do you see an Indian or a White man?"

"I see both," she said honestly, wondering exactly what was troubling him so.

Searching her face, he came a few steps closer until his towel was almost brushing her arm. "I've never known which I am. Everything in my upbringing has denied my Cheyenne ancestry. My grandfather even wanted me to change my name. He said my mother took back the Chambers' name and I should have it, too. But for some reason, I couldn't do it."

She didn't know what to say to him but decided honesty was best. "You can't deny who you are, Mac. I had Jeff's name changed back to Corcoran when I changed mine. But I did that because Robert wanted nothing to do with us. He had me sign papers freeing him of all responsibility toward Jeff and toward me. But…" And she didn't know quite how to say it, but went ahead anyway. "Your situation is different."

Moments ticked by until Mac asked, "Because I'm Cheyenne?"

"Yes," she said simply. "Robert never cared about his genealogy or his ancestors, and I didn't, either. But you… Your father came from a culture steeped in traditions that might have a lot to offer you. I can see why you wouldn't want to give that up."

His gaze was getting that smoldering look again. When his eyes turned to black, they shone dark and mysterious as they did right before he kissed her.

Night shadows played in the room and seemed to envelop them.

"Dina..." Mac's voice was strained.

She didn't know what he was struggling with besides his desire for her, but she wanted to help him. "I like who you are, Mac. You're a strong man with two heritages to draw on. That should make you feel like *more,* not less."

Slowly he rested his large hands on either side of her neck and tipped her chin up, studying every feature of her face. "And you're a beautiful woman who's driving me crazy, whether you're under my roof or in my arms."

Mac's body was still wet, but she didn't care. Nothing mattered except the two of them here and now. When his lips claimed hers, she pressed into him, feeling the hard planes of his body against her, made more erotic by the dampness on his skin that was seeping into her clothes.

He groaned as her tongue met his. She loved the taste of him and the feel of him and everything about him. She laced her hands in his wet hair and he took the kiss deeper, angling his mouth over hers, sliding his hand between them to cover her breast. When he cupped her, she was on fire. Wantonly she pushed against his palm, needing more.

A shudder ran through him and his kiss became more urgent, his hand on her breast more seductive as he found her nipple with his thumb and coaxed it into an erotic bud. When his hand dropped from her breast, she moaned in protest. But then he cupped her bottom pulling her up into him, into the desire that was waiting for her. Their hips moved together in a ritual as old as mating.

Suddenly, bright lights chased away the shadows in the room, and the two of them were caught in each other's arms.

"I hope I'm not interrupting," Joseph Chambers said gruffly, knowing full well that he was, as the overhead lights burned bright.

When Dina would have jumped away from Mac like a startled teenager, his lips still clung to hers. As he held her, she realized he wasn't ashamed of what they'd been doing.

But then he raised his head slowly and released her from his hold. "You *are* interrupting, Grandfather, but we'll excuse you this time."

That sounded liked blatant defiance to Dina. When she gazed at Joseph Chambers, he looked completely astonished. Whatever was going on with Mac was spilling over into his relationship with his family.

She realized she was damp, even wet in spots from Mac's body against hers. Even if he wasn't embarrassed, she was.

"Excuse me," she murmured. "I'll go get my swimsuit so I can be ready when Jeff is." Without another look at Mac, she nodded to his grandfather and left the glass enclosure.

From the look in his grandfather's eyes, Mac knew he was in for an earful. Usually he listened patiently. This time he didn't want to hear anything his grandfather had to say. "I think I'll swim a few more laps." He slung his towel to the chaise lounge.

"You're asking for trouble." His grandfather's voice was stern.

"You mean because I want to buy Trudale Paper Company? It's a risk but a good deal, too, because they're having a cash flow problem."

Joseph snorted. "You know damn well I'm not talking about a paper company. If you want to sleep with Dina Corcoran, sleep with her. But don't bring her here for Thanksgiving dinner, thinking you'll be able to get rid of her easily when you're finished with her."

"I brought her here for Thanksgiving dinner because she and Jeff were going to be alone."

"Did it out of the kindness of your heart?" His grandfather gave a humorless laugh. "I don't think so."

"You believe what you want to believe. I'm going to swim laps." Sitting down on the edge of the pool, Mac jumped in.

"You've got an added dilemma with this one," his grandfather went on as if he hadn't spoken. "A mother is always looking for security for herself and her child. If you've any doubt about it, ask your own mother."

Ignoring his grandfather in a way he never had before, Mac dove under the water. But Joseph Chambers' words echoed in his head and he wondered what they meant.

After Dina, Mac and Jeff finished their horseback ride late Friday morning, she sent her son to the house to wash up for lunch. She'd been ever watchful of him, checking for any sign that might lead to another asthma attack. But he'd been conscientious about taking his medication, as well as using the inhaler, and seemed to be perfectly fine. Mac on the other hand, Dina decided, wasn't fine. He'd roughhoused with Jeff in the pool last night but had hardly said a word to her. This morning, though he and Jeff had kept up a conversation during the ride, she'd felt left out.

After their ride, Mac had shown her how to take the

brush over her horse to groom him, but she'd finished now and closed the gate to the horse's stall.

"How often do you go riding?" she asked as he patted his horse on the rump and came out to the walkway.

"Not as often as I'd like. About once a month. What about you? You took to riding as if you'd done it before."

She smiled. "One summer my father got a job at a family camp in the Poconos. Every day he led a trail ride. I usually went with him."

When Mac would have brushed by her on the way to the tackroom, she caught his arm. "Mac, what's wrong?"

He stared down at her, his gaze intense but unreadable. "I made a mistake bringing you and Jeff here."

She dropped her hand as if the touch of his skin burned her. "Why?"

"Because I might have given you and my family the wrong impression."

She tried to deny to herself that his words hurt her. "You mean you might have given your family the impression that you're interested in me?"

His dark eyes were neutral mirrors, reflecting nothing. "Precisely."

There was a hardness to Mac sometimes that was another facet of who he was. But she'd realized it only surfaced when he felt threatened in some way. What was threatening him now? She knew she was falling in love with Mac, and she was beginning to believe he had feelings for her. But for whatever reason, he wouldn't admit them. In fact, he was finding every reason to deny them.

"If you're not interested in me, then why did you kiss me as you did last night?" she asked bluntly.

"I'm not denying there's chemistry between us, Dina. I simply made the mistake of acting on it again."

His tone, so devoid of any emotion, cut deeply. "I see. So now we're back to being employer and house-keeper?"

"I think that's best, don't you?"

The hurt she was feeling changed to something more tolerable—anger. "My opinion doesn't seem to count. You do what you have to do, Mac. I'll just make sure I keep Jeff's welfare my focus. On Monday I'll take the day and go into Baltimore and apply personally at a few businesses. Maybe somebody will be willing to train me. If not, I should have enough money saved by Christmas to tide me over until I *do* find something worthwhile."

Then she handed him her grooming brush and left the stable, her eyes brimming with tears.

She was in love with Mac Nightwalker and all she had to do was figure out how to live with that.

Even though winter was approaching quickly, Baltimore's Inner Harbor bustled with activity. Mac looked out his office window over the gray water and the complex of shops. The walkways were busy with workers on their lunch hours and tourists who had the Monday after the holiday free. He'd arrived before seven this morning and hadn't gotten much of anything done. The turmoil inside him wouldn't take a rest and kept him from concentrating on work he usually found fascinating.

Though he'd managed to stay away from Dina, he'd

unexpectedly spent most of the weekend with Jeff, feeling more like a dad than a mentor. He'd bought games for his home computer and introduced the seven-year-old to the wonders of cyberspace, including e-mail. Jeff had been fascinated, and they'd had a grand time shooting down aliens and working their way through mazes, as well as e-mailing a college friend of Mac's who lived in England. Yesterday they'd spent some time outside playing ball.

He was growing fonder and fonder of the little boy. And his mother.

Mac *had* to keep his distance from Dina. Every time he kissed her, he felt as if his world was going to explode. Every time he saw her smile, he thought he'd never need to see another.

When his phone buzzed, he was almost glad for the distraction. Picking it up, he sat on the corner of his desk.

"It's your mother, Mr. Nightwalker," his secretary said. "Line three."

Mac punched the button. "Hi, Mother. What can I do for you?"

"I'd like to know how to get in contact with Dina."

He was silent for a moment. "Why would you want to do that?"

"The Charity Guild has organized a holiday fashion show again. We're going to dispense toys and clothes at Christmas to any families who need them."

"What does this have to do with Dina?"

"She told me she was in the fashion industry. The more I thought about it, the more I decided she'd be the perfect volunteer as one of our models in the show. We had someone cancel. Suzette thinks she'd be perfect, too. I'd like to discuss it with her."

"Dina...Dina's a private person and her world revolves around Jeff. I don't know if she'd want to parade in front of a group of strangers."

"Don't you think that should be her choice?"

Yes, he supposed it should be. But he didn't know if he liked the idea of Dina spending time with his mother and sister. "I'll have her call you."

"You won't forget?"

"I won't forget."

"There is one other thing," his mother commented. "Did you and your grandfather argue on Thanksgiving day?"

Mac paused, then answered, "We didn't argue. We just don't see eye to eye on some things anymore."

Mac thought about the box in the attic and the photo albums, but he couldn't talk to his mother about that over the phone. He didn't know if he should talk to her about it at all.

"Just remember your grandfather has your best interests at heart," his mother reminded him.

Mac wasn't so sure that was true anymore. His grandfather might mean well, but he wanted Mac to live his life the Joseph Chambers's way.

When Mac arrived home that evening, he found Mrs. MaGuinnis with Jeff and he remembered Dina had gone into Baltimore for the day. He also remembered what she'd said about looking for another job.

He was talking to Jeff about school and the upcoming Christmas pageant when Dina came in about fifteen minutes later. Practically ignoring him, she asked Mrs. MaGuinnis to stay for supper. They were going to have tacos and there were plenty to go around. But Trudy declined, insisting she wanted to drive home before dark.

Mac got the feeling Dina didn't want to talk to him any more than necessary. The thought rankled, even though he'd been trying to keep contact between them limited, too.

The atmosphere over dinner was strained. Afterward Jeff went to watch TV. Dina had disappeared after she'd cleaned up the kitchen and now he found her in her bedroom, standing on the step stool, attempting to hang a curtain valance.

"Let me help you with that," he said gruffly as he pulled a straight-backed chair to the opposite side of the window, climbed onto it, and took hold of the other end of the curtain rod. In a few seconds, he'd snapped it into place. The valance was a pretty flowered material that added color to the room.

Her gaze locked with his for a moment, then she said, "I finished this before Thanksgiving. I figured I might as well put it up while we're here."

Because they'd be leaving.

Neither of them spoke for a few moments until finally he asked, "How did it go today?"

She climbed down from the stool. "Fine. I have a couple of leads. I need to write up a resumé. Trudy said she has an old typewriter I can use."

He felt guilty because he'd told her he'd teach her how to use his computer. "Why don't you come to my office with me? I'll show you how to use the word processing program on the computer. It would be much easier than a typewriter."

"I don't want to put you to any trouble," she said formally.

Stepping down from the chair, he faced her straight on. "It won't be any trouble. Come on, I'll show you now."

"I have to put Jeff to bed soon—"

"In a half hour I can teach you the basics. You'll pick it up quickly."

She was wearing a pale blue silky blouse with black slacks and looked thoroughly feminine and desirable. But he had to forget about that. He had to forget about a woman who was very different than he was and might only be looking for security...might want to grab the gold ring through him.

A few minutes later, Dina was seated at the desk in his office. He leaned over her, showing her how to use the mouse to open the window she would need from the menu bar at the top of the monitor. His face was very close to hers.

Tempted to turn his lips to hers, he straightened and said, "My mother wants you to call her."

Dina swiveled around in the chair and looked up at him. "Why?"

He told her briefly that his mother was going to ask her to be a model at the Christmas benefit.

After a long silence, she asked, "And what do you think about me doing that?"

"I think it's up to you."

Dina shook her head. "It's not as simple as that. I need to know if you want me spending time with your mother and sister."

"You won't be with them per se. There are a lot of women involved in the Charity Guild benefit."

Although that was true, Mac saw the light in Dina's eyes that said she wanted to do this very much. To start moving in his circle? Whatever the case, this was her decision, not his. "It doesn't matter to me, Dina. Really. But for the sake of your reputation and mine, it would be better if they don't know you're living here.''

She thought about that. ''I'll call your mother and see what's involved. Then I'll decide.'' Breaking eye contact, she glanced at her watch. ''But first, I'm going to put Jeff to bed.'' She motioned to the computer. ''Thanks for the lesson. Is it okay if I try to figure out more of it tomorrow?''

''Sure. You can use it anytime you want. So can Jeff. I told him after he finishes his homework, he can have more fun with the games.''

''Thanks for sharing those with him.''

As she gazed up at him, he wanted to draw her into his arms. But he knew he had to stop considering it. Once she found another job, she'd be gone.

And his life would go back to normal.

On Friday afternoon, Dina sat in one of the meeting rooms in Baltimore's classiest hotel, marveling at the fashions presented to the Charity Guild's benefits' committee. Mac had offered to pick up Jeff after soccer practice so she didn't have to rush home. Dina realized now that this meeting could go on for hours, and Mac must have known that.

Leona sat on one side of her with a clipboard, Suzette on the other, as designer fashions were waved in front of their noses. Lois Myers, the blonde who had accosted Dina when she'd exited the powder room at the cocktail party, was also there, sending hostile glances her way.

Lois asked her now, ''What do you think of that little blue number? It looks like your size.''

Although Lois and Suzette were helping to choose the fashions in the show, they wouldn't be modeling.

Dina studied the pale blue sheath, knowing a deeper shade of blue would be more flattering for her. But she wasn't about to let Lois get the upper hand. "I think it would be perfect with a theme. Crystal, maybe. Dangling crystal earrings, a crystal necklace, bracelets and a chiffon swag scarf...multicolored with darker shades of blue."

"You *do* have an eye for fashion!" Suzette sounded impressed.

"Where did you say you work?" Lois asked.

Before Dina could clamp her mouth shut, a string of words popped out. "I'm between positions right now. I'm looking for something more challenging than my last one."

"Exactly just what did you do in your last position?" Lois wasn't going to let this go.

But Suzette came to the rescue. "What does that matter, Lois? Dina's already proved she's invaluable to us. She was right about making the hem shorter on that coral suit, and her knack for accessorizing is wonderful. We should just be glad she's volunteering some time for this."

Dina felt like a hypocrite as well as a liar. She was here, hoping that some contact she made through this fashion show might lead to a good job. But she hated deceiving Mac's mother and sister. They obviously thought she had a trust fund or something from which she was deriving income. They'd accepted her into their circle. What would they do if they found out she was Mac's housekeeper?

Keeping up pretense was exhausting, Dina thought, as she drove back to Mac's house later that afternoon. But the forty-five minute drive gave her a chance to think about what she was doing and why she was doing it. She wanted to prove to everyone, especially Mac, that even though she didn't have much money, she had ideas and talent that could one day make her a success. It was silly maybe, and a convoluted way to go about it, but this fashion show could be a ticket to take her where she wanted to go. In the next two weeks, there would be meetings with boutique managers, alteration experts, as well as the manager of a modeling agency. Anything could happen and she would be ready to take advantage of it if it did.

As she drove up Mac's driveway, dusk was settling in. Mac had insisted she park in the garage next to his car and even had given her a remote control of her own. It was a luxury she'd never enjoyed before, and she told herself she'd better not get too used to it.

When she veered around the circular drive, she saw a vehicle parked there that she didn't recognize. It was a blue minivan. Maybe it belonged to one of Mac's friends.

In the garage, she switched off the ignition and climbed out, excited about the afternoon, but worried about it, too. What if Mac's mother found out exactly who she was before the fashion show?

Pressing the button for the garage door to lower, she went up the step into the kitchen hallway. There was laughter coming from the kitchen and a voice that she recognized...

Her heart started beating faster. As she stepped into the light of the kitchen, Toby Corcoran came toward her with open arms. "Give me a hug, darlin'. It's been much too long since I saw your pretty face."

Tears came to Dina's eyes. Her father's red hair was tousled, his face more worn, and he looked as if he'd lost weight. It had been *much* too long and she was overjoyed to see her dad. But trouble always followed Toby Corcoran wherever he went.

She wasn't sure she was ready for more of that.

Chapter Eight

After Dina settled Jeff and her father in for the night, she went to search for Mac. He seemed to like her dad, and he'd suggested Toby stay in the small studio apartment above the detached garage. Toby had protested the invitation a bit, then happily agreed, saying he'd like to be close to his daughter and grandson while he was here.

While he was here.

How long would he stay this time? Dina wondered.

But now she had to find out if Mac's invitation had been more polite than welcoming. Her father could take advantage of people, she knew that well. She didn't want him taking advantage of Mac.

She found Mac in the family room watching the news on TV. He was lounging on the sofa wearing a black T-shirt and black jogging pants, one leg crossed over the other. She had to keep reminding herself he didn't care about her. They were employer and employee with an explosive bit of chemistry between them.

That was it.

But when he heard her come into the room, he didn't look at her as if she were just an employee, and that's what confused her.

Switching off the TV, Mac swung his legs to the floor and sat up. "Is the room above the garage okay for your dad?"

That room, with its sink, full bath and foldout sofa bed, was nicer than a lot of places she and her father had lived. "It's fine. But I don't want you to think you have to house him. In fact, maybe all three of us could find another place." Maybe this time her father would stay and they could actually be a family.

But Mac shook his head. "Don't be ridiculous. My last gardener lived up there. It's been empty since then. Why shouldn't Toby make good use of it?"

When Dina had gotten home, after the initial hugs and kisses from her dad, she'd quickly learned that he and Mac were on a first-name basis. "Jeff's thrilled that he's here, but I wish Dad hadn't played Santa Claus this early."

Toby had brought Jeff presents that she knew he could ill afford, though he'd told her in the past year he'd made good money and had even invested some of it. But Dina knew her dad. Once he had a wad of money in his pocket, he couldn't leave it there. He had to spend it. If something he wanted caught his eye, those stock shares would be history.

She sank down onto the sofa next to Mac. "I don't know what to do with Dad sometimes. All those toys he brought for Jeff—"

"Jeff loved them. Your dad apparently knows a kid

Jeff's age likes radio-controlled cars and handheld game sets and every size ball they make.''

Dina also wished her dad knew the virtue of moderation. He'd looked so much older today since the last time she'd seen him. As they'd unfolded the sofa bed, he'd seemed off balance for a moment as if he'd been dizzy, but he'd quickly recovered, saying he was just tired. She hoped that's all it was. Maybe she could convince him to have a physical exam while he was here. She suspected he hadn't bothered with one in years.

''My dad's always been a cross between a leprechaun and Father Christmas, but sometimes he acts more like a kid than Jeff,'' she admitted, needing Mac to know the score.

''From what I've heard, grandparents are supposed to spoil grandchildren.'' Mac's lips twitched with wry amusement.

She could smell the trace scent of a cologne Mac had worn that day. His hair was sexily rumpled and his T-shirt so soft, she could see the delineation of muscles underneath. Their arms were almost brushing, and she had to swallow hard and fight her attraction to him.

''Am I acting like Scrooge?'' she asked, trying to make light of it, to make light of the feelings inside her, to make light of the dim room and the intimacy brooding here.

''Did you see the pleasure in your dad's eyes as Jeff opened each present? I imagine watching kids' faces light up could become a real pastime for any grandparent.''

Mac's words carried a wisdom she needed to accept when her father was around. ''You're right, I guess.

It's just…instead of gifts, I wish my dad would stay with us a while.''

"Surely he'll stay until after Christmas.''

"I never know, because *he* doesn't know.''

Mac's gaze dropped to her lips then. She knew she should stand up and walk out of the room. She knew she should go to her bedroom and lock the door. Not because Mac would try to get in, but because she'd be only too happy to *let* him in.

She made a move to stand, but his hand pressed down on her shoulder, keeping her where she was. "I've missed talking to you like this,'' he said, his voice husky.

It was true. They'd been acting like strangers, and they weren't. They were so much more than employer and employee, and they both knew it.

"I don't know how to act around you, Mac.''

"In spite of my best resolve, all I want to do is kiss you,'' he said gruffly.

The desire in his eyes made every thought in her head flee.

When he leaned closer to her, she murmured, "Mac,'' in a halfhearted protest. But his name faded into a land of right words and right thoughts and doing what was best. As his hand cupped her cheek, as he nudged her closer, as his mouth claimed hers, she no longer cared about doing what was best. She gave her growing feelings for Mac free rein…because they were so new, so precious, so deep. She could see how he longed for family, yet couldn't get close to his. She saw the questions about his father that had kept him aloof all his life. She felt the need in him for more than physical pleasure with a woman.

The urgency of his desire increased with every

sweep of his tongue in her mouth, every glide of his fingers over her cheek, every breath that became shared with hers. With a groan, he pulled her silky blouse from her slacks and began unbuttoning it.

Breaking the kiss, he murmured against her neck, "You make me crazy, Dina. I've never wanted a woman the way I want you."

"I want you, too." Her voice was a throaty, silken caress.

His lips came back to hers again, and then in a matter of seconds, her blouse was completely unbuttoned and he was pushing it from her shoulders. Her body was on fire with everything he did to her. She'd never, *ever* experienced anything like this, this need to be one with a man in mind and heart, soul and body.

Grabbing a handful of his T-shirt, she pulled it out of his jogging pants and ran her hand over the smooth skin of his chest. He shuddered, then sucked in a breath and rid himself of the shirt. With desire on his face and passionate heat emanating from his body, he laid her back on the sofa. As he stretched on top of her, he separated her legs with his knee, and his nimble fingers flicked open the front clasp on her bra.

"It seems as if I've wanted you forever," he murmured.

She loved the weight of him, the heat of him, the desire that wound around her like a wonderful net, capturing her for him forever. She'd never been wanted like this before...she'd never been needed like this before. She could feel it in Mac's fingertips and the rough wetness of his tongue, in the fevered passion of his kiss. Apparently he couldn't deny what he was feeling anymore than she could. Apparently his resolve to be simply her employer had snapped.

He trailed kisses down her neck, across her collar-bone, to her breast. She felt as if she would explode with all the wondrous sensations. As his lips found and closed over her nipple, she arched against him, wanting more, wanting him, wanting everything. His tongue rasped over the sensitive bud, and she felt tears prick in her eyes. She loved this man, she loved the way he'd bonded with her son, she loved his strength, and his gentleness and his passion.

Her hands slid down his chest under the waistband of his jogging pants and he went perfectly still. Her love made her courageous. She cupped him and stroked him until he growled, "Enough, Dina, or you're going to be very disappointed."

"I can never be disappointed in you. Besides, we've got all night."

His gaze locked with hers then, and desire was replaced by something flashing in his eyes that scared her. Suspicion? Distrust? And with his next words, she realized she'd read his expression correctly.

"Were you planning to spend the night in my bedroom?" His tone was terse and almost accusatory.

Her desire and emotions still clouded her thinking. She didn't understand why his mood had changed so. "I don't know. I wouldn't want Jeff to find us in mine..."

"I suppose not." There was a coldness in his voice now. He pushed away from her and sat up, running his hand through his hair. "We do have to think about Jeff, Dina, and what would happen if we continued this."

"Continued this?" she repeated, not understanding.

"We'd have to consider how an affair would affect him."

"An affair?" she repeated, trying to get a grasp on what he was saying and finally managing to do it. "I told you before I don't want an affair. I thought—" The words spurted out before she could figure out the affect they'd have on Mac.

"I know you don't. That's why I stopped. Exactly what did you think was going to happen after tonight?"

Suddenly she felt like the biggest fool on earth…she felt as if all the good things growing inside her had wilted. "I thought…I thought we had feelings for each other. I thought we were expressing them. I thought this could lead to…"

"Marriage?" he asked with almost a laugh. "No, Dina. I don't ever plan to get married. Just as I don't ever plan to sell my soul to the devil."

His words rang in the silence until she could believe he wasn't kidding. She could see he actually looked at both in the same light. The idea shocked her and made her speechless. She just stared at him, wondering what was blocking his ability to love.

Had his father leaving his mother made him this cynical? Had his grandfather's tutelage embedded distrust in him? Was there something else, some*one* else, who had made him think any woman would want his money, but not him?

Mac's gaze fell to her naked breasts then, and she could see he still wanted her. But it was obvious he didn't *want* to want her.

A few minutes ago she hadn't been embarrassed. She'd wanted him to see her and touch her. But now everything was different between them. Quickly she fastened her bra and slid into her blouse, buttoning each button deliberately, telling herself she had her pride. She'd done nothing wrong except to fall in love with a man who didn't know how to love back.

Standing then, she tried to keep her gaze from his bare chest, from the deep, deep brown of his eyes. She wanted to say something scathing, something that would cover up her hurt and the pain of his rejection. But all she could come up with was, "If you have any laundry in the morning, just put it in a pile outside your bedroom door. I wouldn't want to invade your territory or go where I wasn't wanted."

"Dina…" he said impatiently.

But she was already on her way across the room, already fighting back tears, already scolding herself for being every kind of fool.

Mac swore viciously as Dina left the family room. Propping his elbows on his knees, he dropped his head into his hands. He blamed his turmoil on frustrated sexual desire, but deep inside he knew it was more than that. He'd seen the hurt in her eyes.

Still, as he stood and snatched up his T-shirt, he told himself he'd done the right thing, that Dina had to know the score. If she'd been willing after that…

But she hadn't been willing. She wanted more than one night in his bed. She wanted to share a life she could probably become accustomed to very easily.

And what if you're wrong? a little angel on his shoulder asked.

But he ignored the question and the angel.

Instead of going upstairs, he went to his den. He studied every picture on the wall, the bronze on his desk, the questions inside him that needed to have answers. Then he took his wallet out of his pocket and removed a slip of paper. It was Frank Nightwalker's address and phone number. The private investigator who had gotten him Robert Craft's information had located his father, too. Mac had been sitting on it for the past two days, but now he couldn't ignore it any longer.

Checking his watch, he determined it would be nine o'clock in the town of Red Bluff outside of Albuquerque. There was no point in waiting another minute to do this. Picking up the phone, he dialed.

On the third ring someone picked up. "Hello?" a deep male voice asked.

Every fiber of Mac's being froze. He felt numb and tight-chested and overcome with so many emotions he couldn't name them all.

"Frank Nightwalker?" he asked.

"Yeah, that's me. How can I help you?" The voice was strong, though a bit gruff.

"I'm calling…" Mac stopped and took a huge breath. "I'm Mac Nightwalker."

The silence that stretched between Red Bluff and Hilldale was comprehensive and all-encompassing.

"I never thought I'd hear your voice," his father said, sounding choked up. Could that be possible?

"I didn't think I ever wanted to hear yours," Mac said truthfully. "But I decided it was time."

"It's long *past* time," Frank said, clearing his throat, obviously composing himself. "But I don't know if talking over the phone is the best idea. Why don't you come out here for a visit?"

The out-of-the-blue invitation threw Mac off balance. He'd expected his father to be defensive, maybe even unwelcoming. He'd never expected an invitation to visit, and suddenly, he didn't know if he was ready for a face-to-face confrontation with his father. "This is a busy time right now."

"I can understand that," Frank assured him. "With the holidays and all. What about after New Year's?"

Mac could see that his father was right about one thing—talking over the phone wasn't a good idea. He had questions, and he wanted to see Frank Nightwalker's face when he asked them. He wanted to see Frank Nightwalker's face as he answered them.

Stalling, needing to think about the best way to proceed, he responded, "I'll check my schedule for after the New Year and then let you know. I have so many questions."

There was a long pause, then Frank said, "I'll answer whatever I can."

Mac's questions were ready to tumble out, but he held them back. He'd waited this long; a few more weeks wouldn't matter.

An awkward silence prevailed again, but Frank broke it. "I'm awfully glad you called. It's the best Christmas present anyone ever could have given me."

Now Mac just felt uncomfortable. "As I said, I'll go over my schedule and see when I can fly out."

They both fell quiet again until Frank filled the void once more. "If I don't talk to you again before, you have a Merry Christmas, son."

Son. The word shook Mac's world. "You, too," he responded, not able to call Frank Nightwalker "Dad," not knowing if he ever could.

Twelve days before Christmas on a Saturday morning, Dina was washing the kitchen floor when the doorbell rang. Jeff had gone over to her dad's room above the garage to listen to him spin stories. Mac had left before she was up. She supposed he had gone to his office. They'd barely spoken the past two weeks.

She couldn't bear to be around him, loving him, knowing her love wasn't returned. Somehow she had to find armor. They'd be going to Jeff's Christmas pageant in a few days and she'd have to remind herself again they would never be a family. She hoped her dad would go along, too, and help ease the tension.

Propping her squeegee mop in the bucket, she wiped her hands on the oversized shirt that hung over her jeans and went to answer the front door. When she opened it, she wanted to slam it shut again. Suzette stood there, her eyes big and round as she contemplated Dina and her rumpled shirt and jeans.

"My goodness, I didn't expect to find *you* here!" Mac's sister said.

Not sure what to say or do, Dina suggested, "Come on in."

Suzette held a folder in her hand. "These are from Grandfather. He thought Mac would be here. Is he?"

Dina shook her head. "No, and I'm not sure where he is."

"But *you're* here. Just what does that mean?"

Wasn't that a very good question? Dina decided the charade was up, at least with Suzette, and she might as well tell her the truth. She motioned to the living room. "Why don't we sit down?"

Suzette took one of the armchairs and then waited.

For the past few weeks as Dina had become a model for the fashion show, she'd helped in any way she could to make sure the benefit would be a success. Suzette, as well as Leona, had stopped in often to watch preparations shape up. But Dina still didn't feel as if she knew either Leona or Suzette very well.

"It's not what you think," she said now.

"And what do I think?" Suzette asked.

Dina blushed. "I needed a job and Mac offered me one as his housekeeper. Jeff and I are living here for the time being." She nodded toward the kitchen. "In the housekeeper's quarters. Mac and I thought it best if everyone didn't know I was staying here so they didn't jump to conclusions."

"I see," his sister mused slowly as if thinking it over. "So what you're saying is—nothing is going on between you and Mac?"

"I'm his housekeeper," Dina repeated, deciding that was the best way to handle it.

"Well...I can see why Mac kept this from Grandfather, but I guess he kept it from Mother, too. He could have told *me* what was going on."

Suddenly Dina remembered something that was very important to her—the fashion show tomorrow.

"Suzette, I know it's a lot to ask, but I've really enjoyed my work on the fashion show and I want to make tomorrow a success as much as you do. I'm a seamstress, and I want to take fashion design classes. I'm looking for a job in the field, but nothing's come up yet. That's why I'm here. I'd really appreciate it if you could just keep this quiet until after the fashion show. The other women...well...they'd look at me differently."

Suzette's brown eyes studied Dina. "Yes, I suppose they would." After a pensive pause, she decided, "And you *are* very talented. You have a good eye for fashion. I'll keep this under wraps until after the show. But then I can't make any promises."

"Thank you. It means a lot to me."

She stood. "I'll just tell Grandfather that Mac wasn't here, and I didn't want to leave the papers untended."

"I can tell Mac you stopped by—"

Suzette shook her head. "No, don't bother. I'll talk to him tomorrow at the show."

After Suzette left, Dina scrubbed the floor with a vengeance. What if Suzette didn't keep her promise?

You have nothing to be ashamed of, Dina scolded herself. *It's not your fault they think you're living on a trust fund.*

She sighed. How had she gotten herself into this mess? By wishing for a life she couldn't have?

No, by loving a man she couldn't have.

She'd finished mopping the floor and cleaning the counters when Jeff, Toby and Mac all came through the front door. Jeff ran into the kitchen. "Mac says we can go get fast food, then buy a Christmas tree. I told him we always get a tree and it doesn't bother my asthma."

Toby entered the kitchen behind her son, a wide smile on his face, his blue eyes bright. "Apparently these two haven't had French fries in over a week. Me, now, I'm going someplace a little classier."

Dina could feel Mac's eyes on her, but she kept her attention on her father. "You are?"

"I'm taking Trudy MaGuinnis to lunch. I think she likes me."

"Now, Dad, don't you string her along. Trudy's a nice lady and—"

Toby cut in with an even broader smile. "We're just going to have a few laughs, some good conversation. She's the friendly sort and so am I. Why not have some fun while I'm here?"

Shaking her head, Dina finally met Mac's gaze. How could she sit across the table from him and eat burgers when all she could think about was how he had kissed her and touched her?

She couldn't.

There was an obvious solution. "Jeff, I think I'll just stay here and finish cleaning."

"Aw, Mom, you can't," he wailed. "Come on. You've got to come with us. Doesn't she, Mac?"

After a moment, Mac agreed in a neutral tone, "The cleaning can wait."

She could see the outing was important to Jeff, and she would do anything to make him happy. Especially this time of the year. "All right," she finally gave in. "But I need fifteen minutes to get freshened up."

Lunch at a fast-food restaurant and then the search for a Christmas tree was a bittersweet experience for Dina. Jeff kept up a constant chatter, filling in any and all quiet voids while they ate and then drove to a strip shopping center. All types of Christmas trees were lined up in rows in a large lot beside the garden shop. Jeff ran up and down the rows, pointing to exactly which ones he liked best. His excitement should have been catching, but Dina remembered all too well what had happened on the sofa with Mac two weeks ago.

Christmas was a time for special family adventures, for secrets, for traditions. She and her Dad had always celebrated Christmas, but preparations had been few and far between. The past few years, she and Jeff had created their own rituals, baking cookies, wrapping gifts that were more intangible than tangible. Last year Jeff had given her a drawing he had made in school and another box holding a note with five *X*'s and five *O*'s, signifying hugs and kisses. Nothing had ever meant more to her. On her part, she'd made Jeff clothes and found toys on sale. They'd shared Christmas dinner with Trudy.

This year they'd be with Mac, yet they wouldn't *really* be with Mac. It was confusing for her; she didn't want it to be confusing for Jeff.

She said to Mac now, "I could just get a small tree and put it in the sitting area of my room with the TV."

"Jeff would be disappointed," Mac decided, his gaze steady on hers.

A cold wind blew around her and she lifted the collar of her coat around her neck. "He'll be more disappointed if we pretend we're a family and we're not."

After a long silence, Mac stuffed his hands into his pockets. "We can all enjoy a tree in the family room."

"I suppose so," she murmured, trying to convince herself that they could enjoy a tree without being a family. "What kind of decorations did you have in mind?"

He shrugged. "What do you think?"

"Do you have any?"

He shook his head. "I've never had a tree in the house before. It seemed unnecessary when I was there so little."

"Do you mind if Jeff and I make the decorations? I can probably get Dad into the act, too. We can bake gingerbread men and cut out paper snowflakes. If we stop at a craft shop, I can get ribbon for bows."

Mac was gazing at her with that unfathomable expression again as if he was trying to figure out what she was all about. "You'd really go to all that trouble?"

"It's not trouble, Mac. It's part of the season. We can even collect pinecones from the backyard and with a hot-glue gun make all kinds of decorations and centerpieces.''

Mac's expression was gentle as he looked down on her, and she wished the barriers between them would drop away. But he was who he was and she was who she was. Besides that, he was a man who didn't believe in marriage.

The wind tousled her hair around her face and he said gruffly, ''You should have worn a hat.'' He took one of her hands between his. ''You're ice-cold. You need a pair of gloves, too.''

Her hand in his suddenly warmed up as well as the rest of her. ''I have gloves, I just didn't think to bring them along.''

Jeff raced up to them then and tugged on both their elbows.

''I found the perfect tree.''

As Mac looked down at Jeff, he must have seen that the seven-year-old's coat sleeves were way too short and the zipper pulled a little too tight. ''I think you need a new winter coat, one with one of those furry hoods.''

''That was on my list to buy next,'' Dina said lightly. ''The weather just turned a lot colder before we were ready. C'mon. Let's see this tree.''

Jeff pointed out the ''perfect'' tree, and they decided it was just the right one. Jeff was intrigued with the way the clerk put the evergreen onto a special machine that bagged it in netting so they could transport it more easily.

In the meantime, Mac pointed to a children's store in the strip shopping center. ''Why don't you go get Jeff a coat now?''

''Oh, I was going to buy it someplace more...

economical. Besides, I don't have my checkbook with me.''

"No credit cards?"

"They can get a person in trouble. I'm better off without them.''

Again Mac studied her quizzically and then he slipped his wallet out of his pocket and took out a credit card. "Will you let me buy Jeff a coat for Christmas?''

"Mac, no. I can't accept—''

"Look, Dina. I want to get him something he needs. You know Toby's going to have the toy market covered.''

When she still hesitated, he took her hand and placed his credit card in it. "Do you need him along for the size?''

"No...''

"Then while we're loading up the tree, you can find him a coat.''

"But I can't sign...''

"Let me give you a note. I want the coat to be a surprise. If the clerk gives you a hassle, I'll go in. Okay?''

Should she accept his offer or shouldn't she? Jeff definitely needed the coat, but she didn't want to feel as if Mac were giving her charity. He'd done enough for them.

"If you don't buy him the coat for me, Dina, I might have to join Toby in looking for more toys.'' There was a winsome quality in his eyes now, and she couldn't help but smile because she knew that's exactly what he'd do.

"All right. But, Mac, nothing else.''

He looked roguish when he said, "We'll see.''

She shook her head. Apparently Christmas brought out the kid in everyone. She just wished this Christmas...

As Mac moved over to join Jeff and capped his shoulder, she knew her wish would never come true. Christmas was about miracles, but her miracle required a change in Mac's heart.

That was too much to hope for even at Christmas.

Chapter Nine

Mac untied the trunk lid of his car as Jeff and Dina went into the house. He was in so much turmoil he no longer knew if putting up a Christmas tree was a good idea or not. Damn, but Dina confused him. She always seemed reluctant to accept anything from him. Was it an act? If it was, she was very good.

Ever since that night on the sofa when his good sense had finally ruled over his desire, he'd felt totally unsettled. When she looked at him with those guileless blue eyes...

But he remembered Maxine's green eyes and how cold they'd turned when he'd found her out.

Jeff had started Mac thinking about Christmas trees this morning when he'd asked if Mac decorated the outside of his house with lights. Mac had said he never had, and then Jeff had asked, "But you put up a tree, don't you?" As if *not* putting one up would be the end of the world.

Mac had thought about a tree and Dina and Jeff

under his roof and decided maybe the spirit of Christmas would lessen some of the tension between him and Dina. It had. And when he'd seen how Jeff was outgrowing his winter coat…

He couldn't help but want to give to this little boy, especially at Christmas.

Mothers, fathers, kids, Christmas.

All seemed to confound him at the moment.

As Jeff "helped" Mac unload and set up the tree in the family room, Dina took the coat she'd bought Jeff into the bedroom and tucked it into a corner of her closet. She'd wrap it for Mac to give him. She'd found one that was warm and practical and reasonably priced. With the authorization Mac had given her, the clerk had rung up the coat in a snap. Jeff was going to like it, especially the fur-lined hood.

After Dina hung up her own coat, she went to the kitchen where she'd left the other bags. Mac had insisted they stop for lights for the Christmas tree and a few boxes of ornaments. The twinkle in his eye had reminded her of a kid on Christmas, so she hadn't protested. After all, it was his house and his tree.

Once in the kitchen, Dina took the art supplies from the bags and spread them on the counter. She was pulling the twinkle lights out of their box when the doorbell rang. At the door she found the mail carrier.

He smiled at her and handed her a few letters with a heavier red, white and blue envelope on the bottom of them. "That had delivery confirmation on it," he said, "so I thought it might be important."

She smiled back. "Thanks."

As she closed the door, she leafed through the mail to see if any of it belonged to her. Then she saw the name on the priority mail envelope—Frank Night-walker.

Immediately she crossed to the family room. "Mac, I think you might want to look at this."

He'd been eyeing the pine, making sure it was straight in its holder. Jeff was sitting on the floor, looking up wide-eyed at the tall tree.

When Mac came over to her, she handed him the envelope, her heart thumping rapidly, thinking about what a package from his father could mean. Had Mac found his father or had his father found him?

Mac saw the address and stared at the envelope a few moments. "I'm going to open this in my den."

To keep Jeff occupied, Dina motioned to him. "Come on. Let's see if we can make some snowflakes to hang on the tree." She'd bought paper doilies for that purpose.

Fifteen minutes later, as Jeff was attempting to cut out a snowflake with blunt-tipped scissors, Dina still hadn't seen nor heard Mac. Telling Jeff she was going to ask Mac if he wanted rice or a baked potato for supper, she made her way through the house to his den. The door was partially open and when she peeked inside, she saw him sitting at his desk, staring at a letter on his blotter.

When she moved closer to him, he raised his head, and the expression on his face tore at her heart.

"What is it?" she asked, worried.

"They lied to me," he said in a low voice.

"Who lied?"

"My grandfather and my mother."

He looked so troubled that Dina went around the desk to his chair. "That was a letter from your father?"

Mac nodded. "I called him. We only spoke briefly—" Motioning to the letter, he explained, "This is his side of the story. It's too full of gut-level sincerity not to be true."

"What *is* his side?" Dina knew Mac needed to talk about this. He needed to get his own emotions out in the open.

Proving she was right about that, Mac plowed right in. "He loved my mother, but he didn't want to be under my grandfather's thumb as my mother had been all her life. She depended on her father and always tried to please him. My dad felt compromised by that. After four years under my grandfather's roof, he decided he couldn't live that way any longer, and he wanted a life for all of us—away from the family fortune and the family name. But my mother..."

Mac stopped for a few moments and Dina could tell he was trying to see both sides of it.

Finally he went on, "My mother knew Suzette and I would have a lot more advantages if we stayed. I was three, Suzette was a year old, and we had a nanny. My dad says it was hard for my mother to think about taking care of all of us by herself, isolated in an area of the country where she'd never lived before. My dad wanted to go back to New Mexico where his father lived." After a pause, Mac added, "My paternal grandfather died about eighteen months ago. I never knew him."

There was such regret in Mac's voice...such a sense of loss. Dina thought about all of it. "I'm sure it wasn't an easy decision for your mother to make. Not to go with your dad, I mean."

"She let him walk out of her life," Mac responded, his voice strained. My grandfather told him once he walked out he'd never be allowed back in. And grandfather had the money and security team to keep him away. But what I don't understand is my grandfather telling me that my dad *wanted* to walk out. My dad says he wrote letters for about a year, but when there were no answers, he stopped. He got the message. He knew my grandfather was too powerful a force to fight. And he didn't want to put me and Suzette in the middle."

"Maybe it was too painful for your mother to answer the letters."

"Maybe. Or maybe she never received them. My grandfather might have destroyed them."

"Are you going to confront them about this?"

Leaning into the high-back chair, Mac gave it some thought. "I don't know. My dad says it's all water over the dam, and he doesn't want to get caught up in the past again. But he *would* like to get to know me."

"I think he sounds like a man you'd want to know."

Mac looked up at her, then nodded. "When I first read his letter, I was so angry at my grandfather and my mother. But now...I'm not sure what I want to say to them. Or how I feel. I think I need some time just to let it all settle."

Silent moments passed until Dina said, "I know something that will keep you busy if you want a distraction." She knew Mac needed some time to absorb it all.

When Mac's eyes caught hers and there was a gleam of desire, she blushed, knowing what he was thinking. Quickly she explained exactly what kind of distraction she had in mind. "I'm going to stir up a batch of gingerbread men. You're welcome to help do that, or make snowflakes with Jeff.''

When Mac smiled, some of the strain was gone from his face, and she wanted to put her arms around him, snuggle into his chest and ask him to make this a Christmas they'd both never forget.

But then he stood. ''Snowflakes and gingerbread men sound like a great diversion. Let's get started.''

As they left his office, Dina saw him glance over his shoulder at the letter on his desk, and she knew his father wouldn't be far from his thoughts.

The smell of gingerbread men enlivened the air when Toby Corcoran came back to the house after his day with Trudy MaGuinnis. A nice lady, she was. He'd met her a couple of times when he'd visited Dina and Jeff at their other apartment. They'd had fun going to lunch. They'd spent the rest of the afternoon talking at her apartment. But he'd been so damn thirsty... That had been happening a lot lately. He'd lost a few more pounds, too, though he was eating as much as he ever had.

He thought about Trudy again. She'd invited him to stay for supper, and they'd talked about warding off old age. It's a shame he wasn't staying in Hilldale longer. But he had *his* life, and Dina had hers. She'd sure lucked into something good with this Mac Nightwalker. He saw the way the two of them looked at each other. They'd be hooked up in some way in no time, if they weren't already.

When Toby walked through the foyer, Jeff caught sight of him from the family room and called, ''Come help, Grandpa. We're decorating the tree. Mom's putting holes in the gingerbread boys' heads. Mac had to go to work, but he said we could do it and surprise him when he gets home.''

Toby laughed as he shrugged out of his jacket. "I'll go check with your mom first, and then I'll be in. Think you can show me again how to get on the Net? There's some things I want to look up."

"Sure. We can play more games when we finish the tree."

Toby left his coat on a chair in the foyer and then went to the kitchen. Dina was standing at the counter with an ice pick, putting holes in the cookies so she could tie a ribbon through them. Dina knew how to do things up really pretty, he'd give her that.

She looked up at him with a smile. "How was your date?"

"Trudy's a nice lady." Toby took one of the cookies and nibbled on it. He loved sweets and Dina made good stuff. "I saw in the paper there's a model train show tomorrow. I thought I'd take Jeff to it while you're at that fashion thingy. We'll probably make a day of it."

"That would be terrific. Just make sure you keep Jeff's inhaler handy. I have to go to the hotel early tomorrow morning to help everyone get ready, and I probably won't be back until supper time. I wish you could see me in the dresses I'm going to model. They're gorgeous."

"You look good in everything," Toby said with a shrug.

Dina came over and hugged him. "You're surely good for a girl's ego."

When she returned to fixing the cookies he said, "Jeff told me Mac's working."

"He was called to his office for a meeting. You

should have seen him putting the lights on the tree. I think he really enjoyed it.''

"He's a nice guy," Toby replied, fishing for what was going on between Dina and Mac.

"Yes, he is." As she said it, she looked troubled. But then she brightened. "You should see the coat he had me buy Jeff for Christmas. He's a very generous man." Then she froze. "Oh my goodness. I forgot to give him back his credit card. It's still in my coat pocket. I'd better get it before I forget."

Toby was examining the many bows that Dina had tied when she returned to the kitchen and laid the card on the counter. "I'll leave it there with a dish of cookies. Then Mac will see it."

Later that night after Jeff had gone to bed and Dina was going over her notes for the fashion show, Toby sat at Mac's computer, surfing the Net. He'd discovered electronic shopping and it fascinated him. He could buy a few more toys for Jeff and get Dina something really nice.

He hadn't had any money to speak of the last three Christmases to buy either of them anything. Dina deserved so much more than he'd ever given her. But this year, thanks to the generous retired folks in Florida who would pay an arm and a leg to have someone take them fishing, he'd had money to burn. One of them had given him a tip about a technology stock that was supposed to really take off. It had *more* than taken off. It had quadrupled in the past few months. He could buy Dina and Jeff exactly what he wanted. Thinking about Dina and everything he had never bought her, he clicked on the jewelry icon and studied all the pictures. There were so many beautiful things. Which one would Dina like?

Then he saw it. A fourteen-carat gold bracelet. He knew she'd love it. It was fifteen hundred dollars.

Toby thought about his checking account and his new stock portfolio. His credit card was maxed out but his portfolio was more than healthy. He could call his broker on Monday and sell a block of stock to pay for the bracelet. But in the meantime…

With Christmas so close, the online retailer might run out of the bracelet. He wanted to make sure he got one of them. Suddenly he remembered Mac's credit card out on the counter. He could use that and then give Mac the money once the stock was sold. That would make it all real easy.

Not thinking twice about it, he typed in Mac's name and his e-mail address. Jeff had showed him all about e-mail, too.

Toby pushed back the chair and went into the kitchen. Dina was in her bedroom, and the credit card was still on the counter with the dish of cookies. He picked it up. The computer age had sure made shopping easy.

On Sunday, as he usually did the first thing every morning, Mac sat at his computer to check his e-mail. His meeting last night had gone on until almost two, and he was later getting up this morning. In fact, Dina had told him Jeff and Toby had already left to go to breakfast and the model train show, and whatever they could find afterward that might be fun. She'd left, too, after she'd made pancakes for the two of them.

Mac checked his watch. In an hour he'd have to be more formally dressed and sitting in his perfunctory place next to his mother and sister at the luncheon before the fashion show. But this year he didn't mind.

He looked forward to seeing Dina parade down the runway and then through the crowd of guests. He remembered the night he'd taken her to the cocktail party. She'd been a knockout. She couldn't be any more beautiful in a designer dress. But he was looking forward to seeing her in one, anyway.

He pushed the idea of her leaving after the holidays out of his head. He didn't want to think about it. When he'd come home last night and smelled the lingering aroma of gingerbread cookies and seen the tree still lit for his perusal, his throat had tightened and he'd felt as if his house was finally a home.

Mac clicked on the appropriate icons and soon saw that he had five e-mail messages. He recognized three of the addresses, but the other two were from electronic retailers. That was odd. He hadn't purchased anything. Maybe they were advertisements. But when he clicked open one of the letters, he saw that it was a confirmation for the purchase of a fifteen-hundred dollar gold bracelet! He just stared at it for a few astonished seconds, then clicked on the second letter. Someone had ordered two-hundred dollars worth of toys in his name, too.

He remembered his credit card lying on the counter with the dish of cookies last night.

Dina.

There was no way she'd have the money to buy a bracelet like that. Apparently she thought she'd take advantage of his generosity!

Though not as outlandishly brazen as Maxine had been, Dina was a gold digger, too. Obviously she was going to start small and work up.

When would he learn that women couldn't be trusted? His mother had lied to him all of these years about his father, backing up the claim that Frank Nightwalker had abandoned his family. The truth was, she hadn't had the courage to follow him. Then there'd been Maxine.

And now Dina…?

He had allowed her damsel-in-distress routine to fool him into thinking she was vulnerable and needed his help. That gold bracelet was going to cost her more than fifteen hundred dollars by the time *he* was finished with her.

Energized and excited by the preparations for the fashion show, Dina rushed here and there, helping where she was needed. After she'd zipped up a dress for one of the models, a petite woman—who had to be in her sixties—came over to her and tapped her elbow.

"I've been watching you all week," she said.

Dina looked startled, wondering if she'd done something wrong. This woman had been introduced to her two weeks ago as Charise Shappel, the owner of one of the boutiques supplying the models with their dresses. "You have?" she asked.

Mrs. Shappel looked at her through her trifocals. "I noticed you measuring and tacking up that model's sleeves on her jacket." She pointed to a brunette wearing a lime-green suit.

"I was told we could do minor alterations. I took small stitches. They shouldn't hurt the fabric."

Mrs. Shappel shook her head. "You didn't do anything wrong, my dear. I'm complimenting you. You have a real sense of style and color. I heard that you're looking for a new position. What is your specialty exactly?"

"I'm a seamstress, but I'm very interested in fashion design, and I'd love to learn more."

Mrs. Shappel's green eyes appraised Dina. "I could use a good seamstress. I could also use some help choosing next year's inventory. Are you interested?"

"I'm more than interested!" Dina answered enthusiastically.

"Well, good. It's a little too noisy here to discuss details. Come into my shop tomorrow." She handed Dina a business card. "We'll discuss salary and when you can start."

A half hour later, Dina stood on the makeshift stage behind the curtain, waiting for her turn to walk down the runway. She'd been thinking about Mrs. Shappel's offer since she'd spoken with the woman. Maybe she'd be able to move out of Mac's house now.

The thought brought her pain instead of pleasure. She didn't want to leave. But she couldn't stay, either, loving Mac the way she did—not having him return that love. She had to think of Jeff, too. They needed to leave before Jeff became anymore attached.

What if Mac asks you to stay?

She would only be able to stay if Mac's feelings for her had grown as deeply as hers had for him. And after what he'd told her about his feelings concerning marriage—

She loved him. But she couldn't have an affair with him. She wanted more for herself and for her son. She'd wait until tomorrow to talk to Mac about all of it...after she found out from Mrs. Shappel exactly what the position paid. That would definitely direct what decision she should make.

Hearing her cue from the stage, Dina stepped out onto the runway, trying to remember everything about modeling that she'd been taught over the past week. She smiled, holding her head high, first giving a view of the front of her outfit and then the back. She stopped after a few feet and turned again, her scarf trailing delicately behind her. Then she walked to the steps at the end of the runway and she saw the table with Mac and his mother, Lois, Suzette, and two other women.

Mac was looking up at her and his eyes glimmered with male appreciation as his gaze swept over the blue dress with its silk scarf and crystal accessories. But he wasn't smiling. In fact, he looked very removed. Maybe it was the setting. Maybe it was the fashion show. Maybe it was the cameras going off when she strolled down the runway.

As she descended the steps, she heard Lois remark loudly to the woman next to her, "She's Mac's housekeeper."

Everyone at the tables around the runway had overheard the remark. Dina's gaze went to Mac's mother. She looked startled. Suzette looked guilty, and Dina suspected she'd told Lois, though she'd promised Dina to keep her secret.

The woman beside Lois tossed back, "I'll bet she's his *personal* assistant, too."

The implication was clear, and Dina had never felt more humiliated in her life. She knew her cheeks were burning red, and her feet seemed to be rooted to the spot in front of the steps. Her gaze went to Mac, looking for help. For support. For something.

But he let the remark stand. He did not correct the impression that she was his mistress.

Too vividly, Dina remembered the kisses and touches she'd shared with him, the desire that had blazed too hot to handle, the feelings that had grown too deep for her to deny. Why wasn't he speaking up? Why wasn't he setting this crowd straight? Why was he looking as if he appreciated her humiliation as much as Lois did?

Life had given Dina enough hard knocks to make her strong. She would *not* let a woman's cattiness destroy her. This fashion show had invigorated her and given her a way to use her talent as well as find a new job. She wouldn't spoil it. She wouldn't give Lois or anyone else the satisfaction of seeing her crumble.

After descending the runway steps, she was supposed to weave in a specific pattern through the tables. Giving Mac a last look, trying to understand why he was keeping silent, she then tore her gaze from his, squared her shoulders, lifted her chin and took the path leading her through the tables of viewers who were enjoying coffee with their luncheon desserts. She told herself she wasn't going to cry. She wasn't going to give into the weight that seemed so heavy on her chest that it could crush her.

But her mind screamed, *Why? Why had Mac kept silent? Why had he looked so remote?*

After her tour around the room, she exited through a hallway that led back to the stage. As soon as she entered it, her practiced smile fell away and she took several deep breaths. But as she tried to compose herself, she heard footsteps behind her. Recognizable footsteps.

Swinging around, she faced Mac. "Why didn't you say something?" she asked, never feeling so hurt and betrayed as she did at that moment.

"What was there to say?" he inquired in a cold voice. "Even though you're not my mistress yet, you've decided to take the liberties as if you are. When were you going to tell me you charged the bracelet? After our next petting session on the sofa?''

His words made no sense, and she wondered when this nightmare had started. She could see the anger burning in Mac's almost-black eyes…could see it molding his jaw into stone…could see it making his body stance defensive.

Where had it come from? ''I have no idea what you're talking about.''

He shook his head and gave a bitter, humorless laugh. ''You're good, Dina. You almost had me convinced that you were interested in *me,* rather than my money.''

Convinced? She hadn't tried to convince him of anything. She'd thought about trying to convince him that she loved him. But she could see now, that would be an impossibility.

Again her pride came to her rescue, along with her Irish temper. ''You aren't making any sense. I didn't charge anything but Jeff's coat, and that was with *your* permission.''

When he would have spoken, she let her indignation carry her on. ''You don't have to worry whether I care about you or not because I'll be moving out as soon as I find an apartment. Thanks to this fashion show, I've found a reliable job. You needn't be concerned I'll come to you for anything ever again.'' Then spinning on her very high heels, she practically ran from him. She had another outfit to model, and she wasn't about to let him keep her from doing her part in this fashion show. Although her heart felt shattered, somehow she'd get through today…somehow she'd find tomorrow.

* * *

It was after nine o'clock when Mac finally went home. After the confrontation with Dina, he had left the hotel and taken a good, long drive. Then he'd gone to his office. It was the one place where he always knew who he was, what he should do. But today, being CEO of Chambers' Enterprises didn't give him the sense of self-worth it always had. His identity had always been tied up with his grandfather's company. But finding out his grandfather had lied to him—finding out his father wanted to get to know him—had changed that in some way. And so had Dina.

Dina.

How could she look so innocent? How could she pretend she didn't know what he was talking about? How could he have fallen again for an act as old as man?

He drove into the garage, put the door down, climbed out of his car and went through the hallway to the kitchen.

Toby was sitting at the table, reading the Sunday paper. Mac wondered what Dina had told her father, if anything.

Closing the paper, Toby nodded to the steaming coffeepot. "I made some fresh brew." He took a silver flask from his shirt pocket and held it up. "Or if you want something a little stronger, we could share a shot of this. Irish whiskey. You won't find any better."

"I guess Jeff's in bed?" Mac went over to the coffeepot and took a mug from the cupboard.

"That he is. And Dina's locked in her room. Her eyes are puffy and she says she has a headache. But my Dina doesn't get headaches, so I thought I'd wait for you and find out what's really wrong with her."

When Mac didn't say anything, Toby poured a little

more whiskey into his own coffee. "I waited for another reason, too. I ordered some presents for Jeff and Dina from one of those stores on the computer. But my credit card is maxed out. I'm calling my broker tomorrow and selling some stock. I saw your credit card on the counter and used it in the meantime. I hope that's all right."

The coffee Mac was pouring spilled onto the counter. "You *what?*"

Toby's brows arched. "I didn't think you'd mind. Dina told me you'd bought Jeff a coat. I haven't bought her anything nice for the past three Christmases, so I wanted to surprise her. And I figured a man like you would have double the limit I do on my card."

The coffee had sloshed down the counter, and now Mac swore—long, hard and viciously.

"You'll have your money by the end of the week," Toby said in a rush. "No sense gettin' your shorts all twisted up about it."

Mac grabbed a towel and soaked up the coffee he'd spilled on the counter and then on the floor. When he was finished, he turned to face Toby, not knowing what the hell to say. "I got the confirmation on your purchases this morning and I thought...never mind what I thought. I've got to talk to Dina."

Toby studied Mac. "Uh-oh. You thought she did it?"

Mac ran his hand down his face. "It made sense. I'd given her the credit card."

Toby shook his head. "I didn't know they'd send you any kind of confirmation or I would have made a point of telling you before Jeff and I left. Maybe I should talk to Dina first."

"No. Let me handle this, Toby."

Standing, Toby left the flask on the table. "You might be wanting this. If you need me, I'll be over there watching the old movie channel."

Remembering everything he'd said to Dina, Mac saw Toby out the front door and watched the older man make his way to the room above the garage. Then he closed the door and reset the security alarm.

Seconds later, he was knocking at Dina's bedroom door.

"Who is it?" she asked through the door.

"It's Mac."

The silence was an obvious prelude to her answer. "I don't want to talk to you."

"Open the door, Dina. I don't want to wake Jeff." He hated using the threat, but he knew it was the only way she'd talk to him tonight.

A few more seconds passed, and then finally the door opened. She was wearing a blue chenille robe, belted tightly at the waist. His heart twisted as he looked at her. Her eyes *were* puffy, and it was apparent she'd been crying. She was pale and he could see how he'd hurt her, first, by not standing up for her when Suzette's friend had insinuated they were sleeping together, and then by him accusing her of being a gold digger.

She kept her voice low. "We don't have anything else to say. Hopefully I'll find an apartment tomorrow, and then Jeff and I will be gone."

"You don't have to leave. I found out your father was the one who charged the bracelet, as well as a few other things."

"Daddy?"

"Oh, he's going to pay me back. He just told me now. If he had said something when he'd done it..."

Slowly she shook her head. "It doesn't matter, Mac. I guess you've always doubted what I wanted from you. You helped me when I needed help and I'll forever be grateful for that...for Jeff's sake. But now it's time for me to leave. If you don't mind, I have a lot to do tomorrow and I want to get to sleep."

Damnation, he did mind! But he could see he wasn't going to get any place with Dina tonight. He couldn't kiss her when she was looking at him as if she hated him. He couldn't try to convince her to stay when she looked as if she wouldn't listen to another word he said.

"All right," he capitulated. "I'll let you go to bed for now. But this isn't the end of it. We'll talk tomorrow."

For a moment, the look in her eyes tore at his heart. But then it was replaced again with a flash of anger. "I might not have time to talk tomorrow. I'll be too busy packing." And with that, she shut the door in his face.

Mac's inclination was to tear the damned thing down with his bare hands. But his logic told him he had to bide his time.

Returning to the kitchen, he saw the whiskey flask sitting on the table. Picking it up, he poured the remainder of it into his coffee cup. Then he took the mug with him to his den, knowing he might as well keep busy because he wasn't going to get any sleep tonight.

Chapter Ten

It was almost lunchtime when Dina returned home from Baltimore after talking to Mrs. Shappel. She loved the woman's store, and the salary the boutique owner offered was even better than Dina had expected. The insurance benefits were good, too. If she was careful, and if she could find a reasonable apartment, in a year or so she might even be able to sign up for those design classes she wanted to take so badly.

So why wasn't she happy? Why wasn't she breathing a sigh of relief? Why wasn't she rejoicing that her life was getting back on track?

Because she was so heartsick. In fact, she felt as if her heart had broken in two. Mac had let her be humiliated because he hadn't trusted her. Without trust, love couldn't get a foothold.

When she went to the kitchen, she found a note on the refrigerator with a smaller piece of paper stapled to it. The note read:

Dina,

I had to make an unexpected business trip to Boston. I've attached the number where I can be reached. I'll be back in a day or two. We'll talk then.

                                                    Mac

Quick tears stung her eyes and she tried to blink them away. They had nothing to talk about. He didn't trust her. He never had. He never would. How could they build any kind of relationship? Then she reminded herself that Mac didn't want to build relationships because he didn't believe in them.

When she thought about yesterday and everything that had happened, she couldn't wait to pack and leave Mac's house. She had appointments to see three apartments this afternoon. Hopefully, one of them would be suitable. She *prayed* one of them would be suitable.

The front doorbell rang, and she went to answer it. But when she opened it, she found her father. She hadn't talked to him since Mac discovered the truth. This morning she'd thought about going to his quarters above the garage before she left for Baltimore, but she'd still felt so hurt, so disappointed in what he'd done.

The expression on her face must have given away what she was feeling because he said, "Don't look at me like that, darlin'. I didn't mean any harm. I intend to pay Mac for everything I charged."

Turning away from him, she went back to the kitchen, feeling not only betrayed by Mac but by her dad, too.

Quickly he followed her. "Come on now, Dina. You and Mac will get this straightened out. He came back a little while ago to pack. Said he had to go out of town. It was an emergency. Looked real miserable about it, too. He's sorry he accused you—''

"I don't want to hear it, Dad. Just as I don't want to hear *your* apologies. You *always* have an apology. You always have an excuse."

"I don't know what you're talking about, girl. I've always taken care of you—''

Years of missing her mother, taking responsibility for herself early, worrying about her dad and where their next meal would come from some of the time, finally made Dina erupt. "You took care of me? Let's face it, Dad. Most of the time I took care of myself, and worried about when you'd be home—*if* you'd be home."

"I always came home," he insisted, angry now, too.

"Sure, you did. After an all-night poker game. Do you know how scared I was in some of those places all by myself at night?"

"Dina..."

"I didn't mind during the day, but after dark—'' All the hurt inside her bubbled up, but she blinked and kept more tears from flowing.

Then she just shook her head. "One week we wouldn't have enough money to buy bread, the next week you'd hit a bonanza, or a deal would come through, or you'd get a good job. Then we'd stock up until you decided you wanted to move on again. Do you know how hard it was for me to change schools every time you wanted to move? Do you have any idea how I felt my senior year in high school when you told me there'd be money for a prom dress and then there wasn't?"

"The boy canceled his date on you anyway!"

She vigorously shook her head again, needing to get this off her chest…to tell her dad how she'd felt all these years. "No, he didn't break our date, Dad. I just told you that so you wouldn't feel bad. But I'm really tired of worrying about you not feeling bad. I'm tired of not being able to depend on you. Of you not sticking around when Jeff and I need you. This stunt you pulled with Mac cost me more than you'll ever know."

In spite of her best intentions, tears flowed too fast for her to blink them away this time. Her vision swam with them and she turned away from her father, gripping the counter, wishing everything was different, yet knowing it never would be.

Toby Corcoran didn't say a word. He didn't try to console her…or change her mind…or argue with her. He turned and left.

When she heard the front door close, she sat on the kitchen stool and let the sobs come, sure she'd never feel happy again.

At the airport the following day, Mac was glad he hadn't checked any luggage on his flight back from Boston. The management crisis with a company Chambers' owned there had been settled to everyone's satisfaction. He'd hated to leave after what had happened with Dina, but he'd needed time to think about all of it. Hurrying with his carry-on bag through the airport, he headed to the parking garage. He had a stop to make before he talked to Dina. He had to get his own affairs in order before they could get *theirs* in order.

A half hour later, he was sitting with his mother in the formal living room of his grandfather's house.

"I've been in contact with my father, and I need straight answers."

Leona looked reluctant to discuss Frank Nightwalker. "Son, are you sure that's a good idea? I..."

"Mother, I need the truth."

Seeing Mac's obvious determination, she sighed as if she'd known this day would eventually come. "What do you want to know?"

"Did he walk out on you?" Mac asked.

After a long, emotion-filled moment when Leona's eyes became shiny, she shook her head. "He pleaded with me to go with him for months, and I knew he wasn't happy here. But I'd been so sheltered all my life. In a way, even college in Chicago where we met was a safe place. There were still lots of rules and regulations when your father and I went to school there. College wasn't the free-for-all it is today."

As Mac waited, she rubbed her hand across her brow. "After we moved here, Frank wanted me to turn my back on your grandfather and everything he could give us. He wanted me to choose *him* over everything else. I couldn't do that. I couldn't move to a strange place where I didn't know if I'd be happy. I didn't know if I could embrace a culture that wasn't mine. I couldn't give up a sure security and deprive you and Suzette of things you could have if I stayed here."

"You deprived us of our father," Mac said seriously, trying not to accuse his mother of anything, believing she had done the best she could.

"Yes, I realize that now. I thought your grandfather could take Frank's place. But he never could. I'm sorry, Mac. I'm sorry I didn't tell you about all this sooner. Your father did send letters after he left, but your grandfather convinced me it was better to tear them up—not to know what he said—not to respond. So that's what I did. He was determined to keep Frank away from us, determined to convince me I was better off without him. I trusted your grandfather too much, and Frank not enough.''

"And I made the same mistake," Mac said, thinking of his distrust of Dina, feeling a keen emptiness since the fashion show. He'd tried to reach her on his cell phone on the way here, but she hadn't answered. He didn't know if she really wasn't at the house or if she simply wasn't picking up until she was sure the caller wasn't him.

Looking relieved to change the subject, his mother asked, "You're speaking of Dina now, I presume?" Leona's blue eyes were knowing.

"Yes. I acted abominably on Sunday by not defending her. But something had happened and I...misjudged her. I didn't trust her."

"She's *really* your housekeeper?"

His mother didn't look as appalled as he thought she might and feeling that she deserved an explanation, he gave her a quick version of how Dina and Jeff had come to be living with him.

Afterward Leona said, "For what it's worth, I think Dina Corcoran is a homemaker, not a housekeeper. She's a very talented young lady. I admire her for the way she's raised her son and how she's managed on her own. I wish I could have had that kind of courage.''

Mac suddenly realized he'd admired Dina from the moment he'd met her. Now it was time he told her that. "I've got to go, Mother. Dina has decided to move out, and I have to convince her to stay."

Leona nodded as if she understood and saw him to

the door herself. Then she broached the subject of his father again. "Are you going to see Frank?"

When he was away, he'd made a decision about that, too. "Yes. I'm going to call him tonight and try to arrange a visit for after the New Year. I also want to talk to Suzette about him. She deserves the chance to get to know him, too—if that's what she wants. I'll have to have this out with Grandfather eventually. About Dina, too."

He and his mother gazed at each other for a few moments, then Mac hugged her and gave her a kiss on the cheek, murmuring, "Thanks for telling me what really happened."

Her voice was shaky when she responded, "I should have done it a long time ago. But I was afraid you'd hate me. I was afraid you'd think less of me."

Leaning away, Mac shook his head. "You did what you thought was best. That's all any of us can ever do."

His mother's eyes glistened with unshed tears, and she gave him another tight hug.

Then he left...to make things right with the other woman in his life. *If* she'd let him.

As Mac pulled along the circular drive in front of his house, he saw Dina's car already parked there. Peering in the back window, he noted boxes stacked on the seat. Damn. He hurried to the front door and went inside, eager to stop her, knowing somehow he had to.

When he found her in Jeff's bedroom, she was packing toys into a carton.

He'd never expected her to move out this quickly. "What are you doing?"

She glanced at him but didn't stop. "I found an

apartment. We can move in anytime we want. I'm going to take a few things over now and tomorrow move the rest. My old landlord said I can borrow his truck.''

"You can't leave.''

That did stop her, and she looked up at him. "Yes, I can. I've found a good job, and Jeff and I will be quite…happy.''

Mac thought he heard her voice tremble. He thought he saw something in her eyes that said she didn't want to go anymore than he wanted her to go. If he could just break through the hurt he'd caused her…

"Where's Toby?'' Mac asked, hoping he could enlist Dina's father's aid in making her listen to reason. "I didn't see his van parked by the garage.''

"I don't know where my father is. Yesterday he left without a word. All of his things are gone. If he doesn't send you the money he owes you, I'll pay you back every cent with interest.''

Before Mac could figure out what tack to take next, the phone rang. "I'll get it.'' He needed to do something useful, needed to give himself time to come to grips with what was happening with Dina.

But when he answered the phone in the kitchen, he listened and then called Dina. As she came down the hall, he said, "It's the hospital.'' He gave her the handset. "Something's happened to your dad.''

Her face went stark-white and he wondered what had transpired between the two of them. After she listened for a few minutes, she said, "I'll be right there.''

"What is it?'' Mac asked, wanting to share her burden, wanting to help her any way he could.

"Dad collapsed outside of an apartment building on the Northern Parkway. Someone called 911 and they took him to the hospital. He was disoriented…

confused. Something about a problem with his blood sugar. They're trying to regulate it. I've got to get there. I said some terrible things to him. I was so…''

Her anguish was obvious and Mac saw that her hands were trembling. All he wanted to do was take her into his arms, but he doubted if she'd let him— and this wasn't the time for that anyway.

"Come on," he said. "I'll call Trudy to pick up Jeff at school and I'll drive you."

Taking a deep breath, she nodded.

Mac was grateful she at least was going to let him do this much.

The ride to the hospital was silent, and Mac could feel Dina's worry. At the hospital he let her off at the emergency room door and then he parked. A few minutes later, when he went inside and asked where she'd gone, he was ushered to a curtained cubicle.

Hearing her voice, he stopped outside of the curtain.

"I love you, Daddy," she said, her emotion obvious in her words. "You're an old fool if you think I'm going to sit by and let you not manage a condition that could be serious. You're going to have to live with me for awhile. I can teach you what to cook…what to eat—"

Toby's voice sounded weaker than usual when he cut in, "I thought you wanted me out of your life."

"I was upset, Dad. I guess I inherited my Irish temper from you. You're the only father I have and I want to take care of you. I want you to live a very long time. Please, will you stay with me for a little while?"

There was a silence as Toby seemed to be considering what she'd said. But then he responded, his voice deep with regret, "I'm really sorry I messed things up between you and Mac. And sorry about everything else, too. All the years you had more responsibility than you should have had—'' His voice wavered, then he asked, ''Are you sure you want me to stay with you?''

''I'm absolutely sure. I love you, Dad. Nothing will ever change that.''

''What happened scared the blarney out of me. I'm feeling better now, but the doc said he's going to keep me in this place overnight. I can cover the cost. You don't have to worry you'll be saddled with it.''

''I'm not worried. Together we'll figure everything out. By tomorrow I'll be moved to my new apartment.'' Her tone was superficially light.

Toby's voice seemed stronger. ''All right. I'll stay with you if that's what you really want.''

Mac stood rooted to the spot, the reality of Dina leaving his house settling in fully. She'd brought happiness and sunshine and caring into his life. He couldn't do without any of those. He couldn't do without *her*. In the past he'd dismissed the idea of having a woman in his life, one he'd want to take to bed each night, one he'd want to wake up with every morning and see across the breakfast table every day. He'd dismissed the idea of ever needing a woman as much as he needed air to breathe. He'd dismissed the idea of finding a woman who could accept who he was.

The conversation he'd just overheard with Dina and her father filled him with hope. He knew how angry she must have been with Toby. He could only imagine their two Irish tempers clashing. But from what he'd heard, she'd forgiven her dad unconditionally and completely. If she could forgive what Toby had done, maybe she could forgive *him*—not only for what had happened at the fashion show and for his distrust, but for not admitting his feelings for her.

Everything had been different since Dina had entered his life. Not only because he desired her. He'd fallen in love with her!

Simply because he'd made the decision never to fall in love again didn't mean his heart had abided by it. Somehow with her courageous spirit, her compassion and her caring, Dina had knocked down all his defenses and wrapped herself around his heart. He loved her and he had to tell her. He had to tell her so many things.

An orderly came down the hall then, nodded to Mac and opened the curtain. "I'm taking you to your room, Mr. Corcoran." The man gave the room number to Dina and told her Toby should be settled in in about fifteen minutes.

When the orderly rolled Toby's gurney out of the cubicle, Toby saw Mac standing there. He lifted a hand in acknowledgment, and then he winked.

Mac took that as a thumbs-up sign and went to stand beside Dina. "He's going to be all right," he told her.

There were tear stains on her cheeks. "I know he will be. I'm going to make sure of it."

As the orderly rolled Toby away, Mac decided this was about as much privacy as he and Dina could find in the hospital. And he wasn't waiting any longer to tell her what was on his mind...and in his heart.

He closed the curtain around them again.

"What are you doing?" she asked, watching his hand on the curtain as he tugged it shut.

"I need to talk to you, and now is as good a time as any."

She tried to shoulder past him. "I have to go to my father's room."

But when she tried to step around him, Mac stopped her by clasping her arm. "You heard the orderly. Until they get him settled and make sure his IV is running properly and take his blood pressure again, it will be at least fifteen minutes. I have a lot to say in that amount of time, and you're going to listen."

Her blue eyes flashed with silver as she tore her arm from his firm grip. "You don't have the right to give me orders, Mac."

This time he clasped both of her arms so that she was facing him. He didn't want to argue with her so he plunged right in. "I've been an absolute fool. I'm sorry for not believing in you, for letting you be humiliated at the fashion show."

Her eyes welled with tears, and she tried to pull away from him. He saw all the pain she'd felt, was still feeling, but he wouldn't let her go.

The fight seemed to go out of her as she realized he wouldn't let her leave. Blinking furiously, her voice bumpy, she said, "What happened is just an indication of how you look at me. You don't see me as—" She stopped and shook her head, looking down at the floor.

He knew she didn't want him to see her cry. She didn't want him to see how much he'd humiliated her, how much he'd hurt her.

But her thinking was wrong, and he was going to convince her of that. He rubbed his thumbs on her arms, gently trying to soothe her, to persuade her to look at him again. "Dina, listen to me. When I thought you'd used my credit card, it wasn't the money I cared about. I was just hurt because I thought you cared about what I *had*, rather than who I am."

Her chin came up then. "That's ridiculous!"

"Maybe to you." He pushed on, knowing he had to tell her his deepest secret. "All of my life, I wasn't sure who I was. My grandfather wanted me to deny being Cheyenne, but I couldn't, because I saw who I was every time I looked in the mirror. My mother seemed to want me to deny the fact that I'd had a father as much as my grandfather did. It was as if she was ashamed of that part of me, too."

At least Dina was listening to him, so he told her the rest. "And then there was a woman I was engaged to a few years ago. I thought she loved me, but she'd only cared about what I could buy her and the life I could give her. When I confronted her with the bills she'd run up in my name, when I called off the wedding, she told me she'd never wanted to marry an Indian anyway."

"Oh, Mac—"

"I don't want your pity, Dina." Now he knew he had to lay everything on the line and take the biggest risk of his life. "But I *do* want your love. You're a beautiful, courageous woman who accepts me for who I am. And I love you for everything *you* are. I don't want you to leave. Not now, not ever. I want you to marry me. I want to give Jeff a real father, if you believe I can be that. I want to make promises to you that will bind us together for a lifetime."

Her blue eyes were bluer than he'd ever seen them, and she looked absolutely stunned. But he just kept gazing into her eyes, his heart wide-open, his love for her pouring out.

She must have finally seen the truth because a beautiful smile broke over her face and she declared, "I do love you, Mac."

Pulling her toward him, he wrapped his arms around her and lowered his mouth to hers. No kiss had ever been so full of passion. No kiss had ever been so redolent with love. No kiss had ever promised so much.

They clung together, their tongues stroking and caressing, their arms holding tight, their hearts beating as one.

Finally Mac broke away and asked huskily, "Does this mean you forgive me?"

She lay her cheek against his. "I forgive you, Mac. I love you so much."

A whole new world seemed to be within his grasp. But he had to make sure. "And you'll marry me?"

Dina leaned away from him slightly then and took his face between her hands. "I'll marry you, and I'll love you forever."

Taking her hands in his, he kissed her palms one by one and then he drew her into the circle of his arms again, never intending to let her go.

Epilogue

When Easter dawned on a sunny April day, Dina awakened with Mac's arm holding her close against him. His chest rose and fell regularly, and she knew he was still asleep. Studying him, her love for him overwhelmed her as it often did. They'd married on New Year's Day, and every morning since then, she'd pinched herself to make sure her life and happiness were real. They weren't just husband and wife, they were soul mates. She couldn't imagine her life now without him.

Attuned to everything about her husband, she became aware of his breathing changing. Then suddenly, his eyes opened and he smiled at her. "You should be sleeping while you can. We have a busy day ahead of us," he said, his voice sleepy-gruff.

"I know. But I want to hide the eggs in the yard for Jeff to find, and then I have to start breakfast. My dad and Frank said they'd go to church with us this morning."

"Those two are getting along real well."

"You sound surprised."

Looking more awake now, he tightened his arm around her. "I guess I am. They seem very different on the outside, and yet when I talk to them both, they have a lot in common."

She and Mac had honeymooned in Albuquerque near Red Bluff. It was beautiful out there, in a different way than the landscape was beautiful in the East. Mac had reunited with his father, and the years they'd been apart had seemed to vanish into the high desert. She liked Mac's dad a lot and had enjoyed the time they'd spent on his ranch. Now he was visiting for a few days over Easter. Although Suzette didn't remember her dad, she'd wanted to meet him, too. She and Frank had spent the afternoon together yesterday and started the process of getting to know each other.

Dina would be sorry to see him return to Red Bluff, just as she'd be sorry to see her dad go.

Mac's mind must have been following the same train of thought. "Toby told me last night he'll be leaving in a week or so."

She nodded, letting her cheek rub against Mac's shoulder. "I'm going to miss him. But his blood sugar has been stabilized for a while now, and I know he's getting restless. I think he's going to head out West this time. I heard Frank invite him to stay there for awhile. My dad could be a bad influence on him."

"Your dad might learn something about ranching. That might be his next investment."

Dina smiled. "I can't quite envision my dad in a Stetson, but anything's possible." She learned that by seeing Mac's grandfather's attitude toward her change since Mac's showdown with him before their wedding.

Mac had given Joseph Chambers an ultimatum—accept Mac's decisions about her and Frank Nightwalker or become estranged from Mac. Joseph was still crochety, but Dina could see the elderly man respected her husband's decisions, even if he didn't like them. Still she was convinced Joseph liked being a great-grandfather to Jeff.

Lazily, Mac began caressing her hip.

She looked up at him and recognized that gleam in his eye. "I told your mom we'd stop in this evening," she said conversationally, drawing circles on his chest—loving the feel of his taut skin under her fingers. "She told me she has an Easter basket for Jeff. I forgot to tell you." After an evening with their dads, she and Mac had found more exciting things to do than talk when they'd retired to their room.

"A basket filled with imported chocolates, no less," Mac remarked with a wry grin.

Then his grin faded and he said, "Before we turned in last night, my dad told me he'd called my mother yesterday. He doesn't know if they'll ever be friends, but they've forgiven each other for hurts there was no use in hanging on to."

As Dina's breathing matched Mac's, his hand crept closer to her breast, and she felt even more excitement and desire than she'd felt on their wedding night...because now she knew exactly how wonderfully Mac loved...how exquisitely tender he could be with her...how demandingly passionate.

When he bent his head to kiss her, she welcomed him with her body, mind, heart and soul. All of her was his now, just as he was hers.

As always, his touch, his kisses, his murmured words

of love took her to the edge of the sublime and into heaven.

A while later, they lay sated, at least for now.

"What are you thinking?" he murmured against her temple.

"I'm thinking that I want to have your baby."

She felt his startled intake of breath. Then he said, "You like your job. And you just started fashion design class in January. Are you sure?"

Tilting her head, she gazed into his dark, dark eyes. "I'm *very* sure. Jeff would love having a brother or sister, and I can't imagine anything more wonderful than raising a child we created—who's part of both of us."

"Dina…"

She could hear the wonder and gratitude and love in his voice. "Yes?" she asked, hoping everything she felt showed in her eyes.

No more words were necessary. He kissed her again, held her close in his arms, and then said the words she'd never tire of hearing. "I love you."

"I love you, too." Their marriage vows had joined them, their commitment bound them, but their love made each day exciting and new.

Mac Nightwalker was her life and she was his…for forever and beyond.

* * * * *

Return to Red Bluff, N.M.
in August 2001 with Karen Rose Smith's
upcoming Silhouette Romance,

DOCTOR IN DEMAND.

**Separated at birth,
reunited by a mysterious bequest,
these triplet sisters discover
a legacy of love!**

A brand-new series coming to
Silhouette Romance from heartwarming author

CARA COLTER

Available July 2001:
HUSBAND BY INHERITANCE (SR #1532)

Available August 2001:
THE HEIRESS TAKES A HUSBAND (SR #1538)

Available September 2001:
WED BY A WILL (SR #1544)

Available at your favorite retail outlet.

Visit Silhouette at www.eHarlequin.com   SRTWL

Feel like a star with Silhouette.

We will fly you and a guest to New York City for an exciting weekend stay at a glamorous 5-star hotel. Experience a refreshing day at one of New York's trendiest spas and have your photo taken by a professional. Plus, receive $1,000 U.S. spending money!

Flowers…long walks…dinner for two… how does Silhouette Books make romance come alive for you?

Send us a script, with 500 words or less, along with visuals (only drawings, magazine cutouts or photographs or combination thereof). Show us how Silhouette Makes Your Love Come Alive. Be creative and have fun. No purchase necessary. All entries must be clearly marked with your name, address and telephone number. All entries will become property of Silhouette and are not returnable. **Contest closes September 28, 2001.**

Please send your entry to: **Silhouette Makes You a Star!**

In U.S.A.	In Canada
P.O. Box 9069	P.O. Box 637
Buffalo, NY, 14269-9069	Fort Erie, ON, L2A 5X3

Look for contest details on the next page, by visiting www.eHarlequin.com or request a copy by sending a self-addressed envelope to the applicable address above. Contest open to Canadian and U.S. residents who are 18 or over. Void where prohibited.

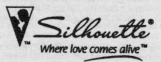

Where love comes alive™

Our lucky winner's photo will appear in a Silhouette ad. Join the fun!

SRMYAS1

HARLEQUIN "SILHOUETTE MAKES YOU A STAR!" CONTEST 1308
OFFICIAL RULES
NO PURCHASE NECESSARY TO ENTER

1. To enter, follow directions published in the offer to which you are responding. Contest begins June 1, 2001, and ends on September 28, 2001. Entries must be postmarked by September 28, 2001, and received by October 5, 2001. Enter by hand-printing (or typing) on an 8 ½" x 11" piece of paper your name, address (including zip code), contest number/name and attaching a script containing 500 words or less, along with drawings, photographs or magazine cutouts, or combinations thereof (i.e., collage) on no larger than 9" x 12" piece of paper, describing how the Silhouette books make romance come alive for you. Mail via first-class mail to: Harlequin "Silhouette Makes You a Star!" Contest 1308, (in the U.S.) P.O. Box 9069, Buffalo, NY 14269-9069, (in Canada) P.O. Box 637, Fort Erie, Ontario, Canada L2A 5X3. Limit one entry per person, household or organization.

2. Contests will be judged by a panel of members of the Harlequin editorial, marketing and public relations staff. Fifty percent of criteria will be judged against script and fifty percent will be judged against drawing, photographs and/or magazine cutouts. Judging criteria will be based on the following:

   - Sincerity—25%
   - Originality and Creativity—50%
   - Emotionally Compelling—25%

   In the event of a tie, duplicate prizes will be awarded. Decisions of the judges are final.

3. All entries become the property of Torstar Corp. and may be used for future promotional purposes. Entries will not be returned. No responsibility is assumed for lost, late, illegible, incomplete, inaccurate, nondelivered or misdirected mail.

4. Contest open only to residents of the U.S. (except Puerto Rico) and Canada who are 18 years of age or older, and is void wherever prohibited by law; all applicable laws and regulations apply. Any litigation within the Province of Quebec respecting the conduct or organization of a publicity contest may be submitted to the Régie des alcools, des courses et des jeux for a ruling. Any litigation respecting the awarding of a prize may be submitted to the Régie des alcools, des courses et des jeux only for the purpose of helping the parties reach a settlement. Employees and immediate family members of Torstar Corp. and D. L. Blair, Inc., their affiliates, subsidiaries and all other agencies, entities and persons connected with the use, marketing or conduct of this contest are not eligible to enter. Taxes on prizes are the sole responsibility of the winner. Acceptance of any prize offered constitutes permission to use winner's name, photograph or other likeness for the purposes of advertising, trade and promotion on behalf of Torstar Corp., its affiliates and subsidiaries without further compensation to the winner, unless prohibited by law.

5. Winner will be determined no later than November 30, 2001, and will be notified by mail. Winner will be required to sign and return an Affidavit of Eligibility/Release of Liability/Publicity Release form within 15 days after winner notification. Noncompliance within that time period may result in disqualification and an alternative winner may be selected. All travelers must execute a Release of Liability prior to ticketing and must possess required travel documents (e.g., passport, photo ID) where applicable. Trip must be booked by December 31, 2001, and completed within one year of notification. No substitution of prize permitted by winner. Torstar Corp. and D. L. Blair, Inc., their parents, affiliates and subsidiaries are not responsible for errors in printing of contest, entries and/or game pieces. In the event of printing or other errors that may result in unintended prize values or duplication of prizes, all affected game pieces or entries shall be null and void. **Purchase or acceptance of a product offer does not improve your chances of winning.**

6. Prizes: (1) Grand Prize—A 2-night/3-day trip for two (2) to New York City, including round-trip coach air transportation nearest winner's home and hotel accommodations (double occupancy) at The Plaza Hotel, a glamorous afternoon makeover at a trendy New York spa, $1,000 in U.S. spending money and an opportunity to have a professional photo taken and appear in a Silhouette advertisement (approximate retail value: $7,000). (10) Ten Runner-Up Prizes of gift packages (retail value $50 ea.). Prizes consist of only those items listed as part of the prize. Limit one prize per person. Prize is valued in U.S. currency.

7. For the name of the winner (available after December 31, 2001) send a self-addressed, stamped envelope to: Harlequin "Silhouette Makes You a Star!" Contest 1197 Winners, P.O. Box 4200 Blair, NE 68009-4200 or you may access the www.eHarlequin.com Web site through February 28, 2002.

Contest sponsored by Torstar Corp., P.O Box 9042, Buffalo, NY 14269-9042.

SRMYAS2